Also by Neerja Raman

**Fiction**

*Moments in Transition: Stories of Maya and Jeena*

**Nonfiction**

*The Practice and Philosophy of Decision Making: A Seven Step Spiritual Guide*

**Reference Chapters**

*Eco-Stacking: A Strategy for Success in Social and Business Agendas*
*(Innovative Approaches to Reducing Global Poverty—Information Age Publishing)*

*Digital Provide: Education Beyond Borders*
*(Streaming Media Delivery in Higher Education—IGI Global)*

# The House on East Canal Road

NEERJA RAMAN

Archway Publishing books may be ordered through booksellers or by contacting:

Archway Publishing
1663 Liberty Drive
Bloomington, IN 47403
www.archwaypublishing.com
844-669-3957



ISBN: 978-1-6657-1691-8 (sc)
ISBN: 978-1-6657-1692-5 (e)

Library of Congress Control Number: 2021925691

Print information available on the last page.

Archway Publishing rev. date: 01/18/2022

To Dadaji.

Lala Bishamber Das
assistant Engineer
Retired
29. D.A.V. College Road
Karan-pur
Dehra. Dun

"Let My Country Awake"

Where the mind is without fear and the head is held high;
Where knowledge is free;
Where the world has not been broken
up by narrow domestic walls;
Where words come out from the depth of truth;
Where tireless striving stretches its arms towards perfection;
Where the clear stream of reason has not lost its
way into the dreary desert sand of dead habit;
Where the mind is led forward by Thee into
ever-widening thought and action;
Into that heaven of freedom, my Father, let my country awake.

The original Bengali poem, "Chitto Jetha Bhayashunyo," written by Rabindranath Tagore (1861–1941), was published in 1910 and was included in the collection Gitanjali. Tagore, recipient of the Nobel, returned his knighthood for "Services to Literature" to protest the 1919 Amritsar Massacre.

# CONTENTS

## PART III: ISHAAN



## PART IV: ANITA

# AUTHOR'S NOTE AND ACKNOWLEDGMENTS

One day, when I was young and impressionable, I yanked at the drawer of an ornate writing desk, a family heirloom, and it broke.

"I didn't do it, Papa."

"Yes. I know," he said. "Your Dadaji did."

My grandfather toured on horseback all over Punjab—some parts are now in Pakistan—building canals, and everywhere he went, that desk went with him. It was designed to collapse into three easily reassembled pieces. Only a camel could carry that much weight, so it traveled in a carry-bag intended to accommodate a pacing gait where both legs on one side move together. It protected the animal and the desk. Thus, his precious cargo, a symbol of dignity and authority, withstood vagaries of several dusty journeys without mishap.

This story, so illustrative of my grandfather's time, seeded a burning curiosity in my heart. The desk is gone. What remains is a hunger for truth. Many questions come to mind. With relics, whether it is the Bronze Age sophisticated water-filtration reservoirs at Dhola Vira, King Ashoka's edicts engraved on pillars made of iron that does not rust, Badami's stone carvings that sing, palaces of Rajasthan, or newer monuments like Taj Mahal, the common historical purpose that runs through the ages is to evoke curiosity with proof of past grandeur.

When visiting the ruined city of Vijayanagar, a capital for more than two centuries in ancient India, I asked myself, *Where would my grandfather's contribution be if he lived in that age?* Perhaps the Queen's Bath with its intricate canals that provided running water? Or the Elephant Stables with their palatial design?

I thank the Archeological Survey of India because their artifacts evoked curiosity about a past that has shaped my present. It is the genesis of this book. The Chand family is fiction. However, three generations of Chands, with their diverse dispositions and evolving ideologies, embody facts, and they epitomize the emotional strength that led to India's freedom in 1947. Relics reconstruct lifestyles of power; *The House on East Canal Road* is a living monument to people whose power lay in principles.

I am indebted to Raj Kanwar, journalist and author of *Dateline Dehradun: The School Town of India*, volumes I and II for his research and for permission to use an image from his collection. Thanks to Shiv for sharing his knowledge about the British Indian Military, to Kalpana for all things avian, and Arun for contributing to Anita's poem. Several authors, including R. K. Narayan, Shashi Tharoor, Amartya Sen, and Gurcharan Das, have informed my work; I am grateful. But mostly I have relied on experiences and memories, since what is documented of the British and Mughal era is the narrative of relics built on conquest. Finally, I thank my editor Elizabeth and the team at Archway.

There is no *am* without f-*am*-ily. I am blessed with the best of the best.

And most of all, thanks to Vasan, my one true heart, who taught me the meaning of love. To paraphrase Kishan Chand, I would be nothing without you.

# PART I
## *Kishan Chand*

# 1

## *Doon Valley, 1905*

In the year 1905, at the peak of his profession, a youthful forty-something Kishan Chand Das hit rock bottom in life. If anyone were to have seen him that day—his immaculate, imposing, six-foot physique crumpled into an incoherent, disheveled, sobbing ball—they would never have believed him capable of excellence in any endeavor, let alone acknowledge his exalted position as the king of the Doon Valley.

But no one saw because Munshi Ram allowed no one beyond the reception hall of Radha Vilas.

The Doon Valley, cradled in the foothills of the Himalayas, protected by the mighty rivers Ganga and Yamuna on either side and bounded by the Shivalik mountains in the south, is home to Dehradun. Two decades ago, when Kishan Chand arrived,

Dehradun—fertile paddy fields, tea gardens, and lush forests—used to be a sleepy settlement of a few thousand Hindus, Muslims, Parsis, and Christians of European origin. The town, though small, was popular with the British as a depot for municipal revenue collection. It served as the cold-season headquarters for its staff, who in the hot season decamped to the Mussoorie Hills, some twenty miles away and five thousand feet higher.

By now, in 1905, Dehradun boasted a fine Forest Research Institute, thirteen schools with more than a thousand pupils, and a cantonment that housed two battalions of Gurkhas who later, in the Great War of 1914, unwaveringly gave life and limb for the Raj. Das Builders and Engineers Ltd., founded by Shri Kishan Chand Das, was the largest employer in the valley. Kishan Chand—his wealth now at par with many a raja—was an acknowledged community leader who also maintained cordial relations with the British. They valued his business.

In awe of his stature, if locals called him Lalaji, Kishan Chand would laugh and say, "The credit goes to Radha. I would be nothing if not for a promise I made to her long ago."

Indeed, his destiny had no parallel. He started by designing canals suited to the unique Doon geography and then laid underground pipes that flowed sweet water from the Himalayan foothills of Mussoorie to the valley floor. He expanded the canal network till there were more waterways than roads in Dehradun. As more people migrated to the valley, Kishan Chand parlayed his reputation for brilliance in designing canals to excellence in construction—roads, buildings, barracks, bungalows—till an entire mile on East Canal Road sported Das Company offices and residences for its employees, who repaid Kishan Chand with undivided loyalty.

Kishan Chand's home sat on two lush acres. The central building blended Haveli architecture—three stories tall; a tree-lined, jasmine-scented inner courtyard that easily held ten *charpais*; a sizeable sitting room—with a colonial veranda wrapping the entire front façade.

A stable, cowshed, and carriage house occupied the back. Large enough to hold a wedding, his house on East Canal Road drew envy and admiration in equal measure.

"If not for my beloved Radha, I would be nothing," he said.

"It befits a man of his stature to be humble," they said.

Dehradun became a jewel in the crown of Doon Valley, queen of the Himalayas. Canals provided sustenance to basmati fields and a cool breeze year-round. On roads that ran parallel to waterways, townsfolk strolled with evening camaraderie; tongas transported children to schools and women to bazaars. Horses drank at regularly spaced troughs, flour mills powered by waterfalls dotted the scene, and dhobis washed clothes at designated outlets. People flocked to the valley.

Infrastructure projects were launched to accommodate growth. Das Builders, supervised personally by Kishan Chand, built the railway depot. The first train rolled into Dehradun Station on March 1, 1900. The British celebrated with whiskey in the Whites Only bar on Platform One, and the town felicitated Kishan Chand and feasted at the house on East Canal Road.

Erect, groomed to perfection in a crisp white dhoti and kurta, a gold-bordered sash looped around his left shoulder, wherever Kishan Chand went, his calm, confident stride radiated purpose.

"For Kishan Chand," they said, "nothing can go wrong."

# 2

*Dehradun, August 24, 1905*

That fateful day began like any other.

By seven, bathed and dressed, Kishan Chand had entered the pooja room, sat on the mat, and was already halfway into reciting the forty verses of the Hanuman Chalisa when Radha slid in beside him. She started her routine by singing an ode to Parvati. She undressed a twelve-inch brass statue of the goddess and poured a tablespoon of holy Ganga water that collected in the shallow lotus-shaped bowl beneath. She then lit an incense stick. Kishan Chand inhaled her freshly bathed sandalwood soap presence and slowed his recitation to allow enough time for her to dress the goddess in fresh clothes, put it back on the carved pedestal, and apply red *sindoor* powder on her forehead where she parted her hair.

They finished together, exhaling om, hands folded in a namaste, heads bowed to end the prayer session.

As they rose, Radha sprinkled droplets of the goddess's bathwater on him, herself, and the air around them till it was all gone.

"Gandhari has a stomachache. I went to see her," Radha explained with twinkling eyes.

Kishan Chand feigned severity. "You should not go to the *gaushala*. What if she kicks you?" Kishan Chand knew Radha visited the cowshed every morning, despite his directives. "You are not your sprightly self these days," he said, unable to hide his relief, "if I may say so."

"You worry too much. And you go to see the horses too." She pulled aside her sari *pallu* to expose an enlarged stomach. "The baby enjoys going to see the cows with me. See how it is rolling from one side to the other?"

Kishan Chand kissed his palms and then laid them on her belly. "This one is for the baby." He grinned. "And now this for you." They hugged for a long minute in the pooja's private room. And then, arms intertwined, they entered the dining room for breakfast to start the day.

As usual.

She chattered away as he drank the crushed almond and cardamom–flavored milk, ate the potato-stuffed paratha she served hot off the fire, washed it all down with water, and rose to wash his hands.

Before leaving for work, he stole a quick kiss. "Not you—it's for the baby," he said before she could object or bring up the problem of prying eyes.

Impossible as it seemed, Kishan Chand loved his wife more every day.

Raised on neighboring farms, he could not remember a time without her. They studied together, played together. He did not know how old he was the first time he took her behind the mango tree, away from parental oversight, and kissed her. She had kissed him back, shyly first, then hungrily.

When he left for college, he said, "You will wait for me, Radha, won't you?"

"What if that landowner's son sends a marriage proposal? He follows us around in the fields, looking at me." Radha's words teased, but she moved close, eyes brimming with mischief, intertwined her fingers with his, and asked, "Have you seen his haveli, Kishan?"

"I will build you a huge house—bigger than his old-fashioned pile. Besides, he is an illiterate lout; he will bore you to death. And he will not take you sidesaddle on a horse like I do. No. You cannot marry him." Kishan Chand encircled her waist with his arms, leaned in, and whispered, "It is decided."

Face buried in his chest, giving tiny kisses, she moved her head side to side, teasing, "No, I can't wait. No promises."

"Say yes, or I won't let go." Kishan Chand tightened his hold. A tussle ensued. Radha never said yes. But her eyes and lips did. The day he left for college, she cried. He kissed away the tears right in front of her aged parents, who looked away from such shameless lack of self-control but did nothing to stop him.

During Kishan's college years, Radha's father had to suffer noisy tantrums when he brought her a marriage proposal.

"Boys change when they go to college," her mother reasoned. "You are foolish to refuse such a magnificent prospect, waiting for Kishan."

But Radha would not listen.

Kishan Chand finished the four-year engineering curriculum in three and came back home to claim his bride. Their marriage—a simple ceremony performed right under the mango tree where it all began—befit their meager finances but not their devotion to each other. Contrary to custom, the love match received parental blessing, and following their cue, the priest also pronounced the union propitious.

How was it possible to love her even more today than he already did?

"Munshi Ram will bring your lunch. I have a surprise planned for you," Radha called from the kitchen, breaking his reverie. She walked with him to the front gate and waved.

At noon, when Munshi Ram came, the surprise was not the one she had planned. "Babuji—come home. Quickly. Bibiji is asking for you. Her water has broken."

By the time he reached home, the *dai* and other attending women had already taken Radha into the maternity room. As was customary in those days, he was not allowed in. "It is too late for you to see her now. Do not worry. Bibiji will be fine,'" the midwife said.

Kishan Chand paced outside the room. He knocked on the bolted door, but—as if in answer—a small scream came through. Then short shrieks, periodically punctuated by long silences. It went on for hours.

Unable to help, he pretended the screams, though different from her previous deliveries, sounded normal. The screams grew weaker and weaker till there was complete silence.

Then the definitive cry of a newborn escaped through the door. He sighed with relief.

No. Something was wrong; no joyous sounds came through the door.

"Let me in. Now." He banged the door till the bolt slid open.

"You have a son," the dai said. She held out a tiny bundle. She had not had time to clean the blood or change the sheets.

Kishan Chand pushed her aside and ran to the bed.

"Radha, say something. Talk to me." He murmured endearments, kissing hands and face, and clung to the lifeless form.

The dai called for help, and Munshi Ram rushed in.

Kishan Chand did not eat; did not sleep; did not allow anyone to move him from her bedside that day.

He did not hold his newborn son.

At night, with some help, Munshi Ram carried Kishan Chand out of the maternity room and put him to bed in his own chambers. Kishan Chand refused to meet anyone, lying sightless, soundless.

In his capacity as a personal manservant to the master of the house and the mistress not being alive, Munshi Ram was forced to take charge of the tragedy. He began rituals for the thirteen days of mourning; proprieties befitting their position had to be followed. Such was the efficiency of the Das retainers that without undue mishap or mayhem, pundits performed poojas; guests were fed and housed. Children were kept busy and away from activities relating to the body, the procession to the cremation grounds, and the cremation itself.

A wet nurse was hired. The baby became pink with health, clenched tiny fists, and opened his eyes.

When he finally emerged, Kishan Chand was man enough to cry in front of all. Matchmakers presented marriage proposals.

"How will you manage, Lalaji?" said women wanting a share of his wealth and youth. "You need a woman's guidance, or they will rob you blind. How long before the milkman mixes water in the milk? Who is to order the rice, get wheat stocks replenished? And what about this huge *kothi*? After every monsoon, leaking roofs must be plugged and walls whitewashed. A big household like yours has many expenses."

Kishan Chand had never needed to know the effort entailed in maintaining Radha Vilas or its large number of residents.

Traditional women paraded daintily and smiled from the safety of a veil. Anglicized women openly tut-tut-ed at his folly of stoicism. Envious men feigned concern.

"Such a loss, and that too at the peak of your manhood. You are young enough to father more sons, and you have money enough to feed a *biradari* clan."

"I will not marry again." Kishan Chand desired no more sons. Including the newborn, he already had four.

"How about a daughter? You have no daughters," they said.

Kishan Chand poured *havan samagri* into the holy fire when pundits indicated. "I have been luckier in love than any man has a right to be. It will fulfill my lifetime of wants. Another marriage would destroy precious memories."

But among the townsfolk, the debate raged: marry or not?

When he could handle it no more, Kishan Chand retired to his chambers. Only Munshi Ram had permission to enter.

"It is the tenth day since Radha Bibi passed. Why not go to your office today. It will distract you," said Munshi Ram, desperate to get him out and about.

"I lived for Radha. Why should I go to work? Anyway, the British have betrayed me. Hypocrites! I thought we were partners."

"Why? What happened?" Munshi Ram was happy to hear him talking.

"Last month, the *Imperial Gazetteer* announced Curzon's plan to partition Bengal. I went to see the Laat Sahib. We meet regularly, and I thought him a good man. I said the partition would foment division along religious lines and urged him to use his influence with the viceroy to stop its implementation." Kishan Chand paced. "Do you know what he said?"

"No. What did he say?" Munshi Ram was afraid to ask, but at least Babuji had stopped holding his head in his hands. Angry was better than lifeless.

"He said, 'Mr. Das, do what you are good at; leave ruling the country to the British. You Indians do not have the discipline to manage yourselves. If you meddle in my business, there will be consequences to yours.' Can you believe it? He threatened me. I thought he would help; instead, he parroted government propaganda."

"What about Manager Sahib?" Munshi Ram pleaded. "He asked to see you."

"If I go to work, it will be to organize a walkout. So, better for him if I don't go."

"Yes—maybe a bit more rest." Munshi Ram abandoned the topic.

Kishan Chand settled into a deeper funk. Documents requiring attention were sent by the office, but he flung them aside: unopened, unread, unsigned. Munshi Ram gathered them, and the pile grew.

One morning, a classic postal-pink envelope arrived—a telegram. Kishan Chand turned it over and over, afraid of more bad news.

"Who is it from?" asked Munshi Ram.

Kishan Chand, lost in thought, pocketed the paper, patted it secure, but did not reply.

On the fifteenth day of his wife's death, two days after the pundits permitted travel, Kishan Chand announced he was leaving town.

"My house is yours, so stay as long as you want, but I have to go."

He gave no directives on what was expected from them or what his plans were. Indeed, Kishan Chand hardly knew himself. All he knew was, without Radha, he could not abide Radha Vilas.

# 3

## *Allahabad, 1905*

Kishan Chand boarded the Dehradun-Allahabad Express by mounting all three steps from the platform to the bogie with one upward swing of his right leg. He walked in, locked the door, and looked around: empty. Not surprising since he had bought every seat—first class was not for whites only; they needed his money—but still a relief. Rajas and nawabs routinely booked entire trains when they wished to avoid the white man, so a compartment to himself was well deserved at such a troublesome time.

The mahogany interior—clean symmetrical lines, padded leather seats, side panels adorned with windows, a pair of cream-colored, operable sash decorating each curtain—soothed his nerves; the coach, designed and built by the American Car & Foundry

Company, had been his procurement when Dehradun was connected to Hardwar Junction. His temper improved a tad.

The train whistled its departure. As it picked up speed, feeling safe from the possibility of any human encroachment, Kishan Chand sat and exhaled tension. For the first time since that fateful day when Radha died, the clanging in his brain softened; waves of relief coursed through his body. It was not that his wife's death had launched additional responsibilities, but her death left a void, a lack of purpose. *Why should I awaken every morning?* Kishan Chand took out the telegram from his breast pocket and, though he knew it by heart, read:

> By the grace of God we are blessed with a girl STOP
> Mother and child healthy STOP Me ecstatic STOP
> Visit us if possible STOP Moti Lal Tripathi

Moti Lal, his friend from college, was a lawyer in Allahabad High Court. They kept in touch by announcing births and significant family events, but it had been years since they had met. Every Diwali, greeting cards enclosed in a gift box—sweet *mithai*, savory *pakwans*, cashew nuts—were exchanged to convey goodwill.

*A daughter ...*

Moti Lal's first child was born after many years of marriage. A favorable time for him. How to announce his own misfortune in the face of such joyful news?

A telegram?

> Wife dead STOP Self grief-stricken STOP Happy
> for you STOP Kishan Chand Das

Or, a letter?

Dear friend, Congratulations on your good fortune.
I unfortunately must announce …

Ruefully, his inability to pen a meaningful missive had resulted in the trip to Allahabad. Words could not convey joy and devastation in the same breath without sounding false. But a visit—that seemed much easier. In person, he could express joy at Moti Lal's good fortune while grieving his loss.

And disappear from Dehradun.

On board the train, the morning's frenzy—packing, gifts, last-minute reservations, horses hurtling—faded. The lull in action deadened his spirit. Family, prestige, money—everything he strove for—was motivated by Radha. She was his reason for living, his companion, confidante, friend, and lover. She understood he was quick to anger but easily appeased and compensated for his erratic behavior with kindness and humor. If his analytical criticism of an employee caused hurt, she mitigated it with a gift basket. An unnecessarily harsh reprimand of a child she hugged away, and his disinterest in a visiting relative she diffused with lavish hospitality. *I enjoyed support of the Indian community because of Radha.*

As for the British, a jaded stare at the lavish compartment brought home his complicity in their agenda. They guaranteed an Englishman investing in Indian Railways returns double those from British government stocks, funded by taxes levied on Indians. Money generated in India flew directly to the queen's backers. High-level railway jobs were reserved for whites and paid from ticket revenue. They gave Indians unskilled jobs at meager wages. A façade of the railways as a bulwark of British pomp and glory kept platforms picturesque: red kurtas held at the waist with black belts for coolies and khaki pants and shirts decorated with brass buttons for cleaners. Englishwomen admired paintings of this marvel without knowing that they docked the cost of uniforms at source from paltry wages.

Kishan Chand wondered how he could have so been blind. Das

Builders and Engineers was guilty of filling colonial coffers. He slumped into the cushions, and eventually, massaged by the gentle rocking motion of the train, he rested. The bed proved comfortable. He dreamt. A daughter! How fortunate for his friend.

Moti Lal was celebrating Dasoothan, the tenth-day ritual of his daughter's birth, with elaborate ceremony when Kishan Chand knocked on the front door.

"You always had great timing," said an elated Moti Lal, tripping over the threshold in a hurry to greet his friend. "Prayers are over, and pundits have feasted on our traditional cuisine—*kaddoo, kachori, raita,* and *halwa*—with lip-smacking approval. Come in. Come in. Why are you glued to the doorstep?"

Moti Lal led the way to an inner room, deposited the small suitcase, and indicated a place to wash. "Hurry. Not a minute to lose. I still cannot believe this miracle in my life."

Buoyed by Moti Lal's obvious delight, the scent of marigolds, the beauty of mango-leaf garlands, and the festive atmosphere, Kishan Chand shelved his sorrow and the nagging thought that his reason for coming was something other than felicitating his friend's fortune. It helped that Moti Lal still looked like he did in college. As they chatted, the intervening years slipped away, replaced by an intimacy of youthful, carefree days when every joy was shared.

"Kishan, don't worry about having a bath. I will check with my wife to see if she is ready and be right back to fetch you."

They tiptoed in. The baby slept soundly in her mother's arms. Though tightly swaddled, she had pulled out a fist, which was lodged firmly into her tiny pink mouth with a determination that belied her tender age. Dark black curls framed long lashes that cast a shadow on plump cheeks.

"I cannot believe my eyes," marveled Kishan Chand. "You

certainly have done nothing to deserve such an angel. It must be Bhabhi's karma that you are so blessed."

"No argument there, Kishan. Your Bhabhi is indeed the worthy one."

Kishan Chand did not know what impulse drove him to utter his next words. "Will you allow your daughter to be a bride for my son?"

Moti Lal laughed out loud. Bhabhi smiled at such audacity.

But Kishan Chand did not apologize for his reckless words. Instead, he dove in further. "I am serious, Bhabhi. Moti Lal, do you accept my offer?"

"I don't know. Which son did you have in mind?" Moti Lal joked to ease the tension. "I know you have several, but do you have one of suitable age? You know the right age difference—not too much, nor too little—makes for a compatible union."

Kishan Chand had not yet thought that far.

It was not unusual for friends to build a bond through the promise of matrimony between young children because marriage within one's own extended family was forbidden by *gotra*—the Hindu genealogy rule of who may wed whom, instrumental in preventing genetic malfunction. It meant that the role of matchmakers gained importance since they made it their business to go across cities and household to track births, horoscopes, and ages of offspring. For them, no age was too young to propose a match they deemed suitable. However, matchmakers, though necessary, could not be relied on for the best guidance, so whenever possible, friends took matters into their own hands and proposed alliances. This also meant pledging troth sooner rather than later to avoid disappointment of a prepledged child. By now the idea was firmly lodged in Kishan Chand's heart. Though untimely, it was not an unreasonable proposal.

"Good question, Moti Lal. I am indeed blessed with strapping sons, and I have no answer at this moment. But I promise to put your interests above mine in selecting a son for your daughter."

Moti Lal looked at his wife, and she gave the briefest of nods.

"Okay, I will talk to your Bhabhi." Moti Lal wrapped his arms around Kishan Chand's shoulders and ushered him out of the nursery. "I know no better man than you, my friend. And certainly, genetics is in your favor; you must have fathered talented sons." A friendly cuff reinforced the thought as he led the way to the *baithak*, formal sitting room.

Kishan Chand continued to look disheartened. Moti Lal, thinking it was because of the delay in agreeing, expanded on the matter of suitable sons. "My college days remind me you are a stickler for education. I may never have passed law school if it was not for you riding herd over my study schedule. Remember how I would sneak out for an after-dinner paan and cigarette, and there you were—hustling me back."

They found the baithak quiet; the guests gone.

"You must be starving, Kishan." Moti Lal called for the cook. "Let us eat kachoris and hear your news. My daughter is indeed lucky for me since she has brought you into my life again, but I was hoping to meet Radha Bhabhi too."

With every piece of roti dipped in *daal* and sabzi that went into his stomach, Kishan Chand unburdened his heart.

"Tell me, why should I live? Without Radha, what purpose do I serve?"

"Now you are not only father but also mother to your sons. They will emulate you. If you wallow in self-pity, so will they; if you accept your fate, so will they. And what about your business? If you let the Bengal partition ruin your finances, then surely the Raj would have won. Plus, your contributions to science are exactly what India needs for self-reliance. Didn't you tell me once that your engineers designed such an efficient rail engine that the British got scared and transferred such new development to England?"

"The house on East Canal Road eats away at my memories, and the office reminds me of the governor's insult."

"Okay. You cannot return to Dehradun in your current frame of mind."

"But I don't want to stay here and burden you either."

"Finish your lunch and rest. You are tired. I will think of a solution. Allahabad is named Prayagraj because people from all over the world come here to rejuvenate. You too will heal enough to approach life with dharma and a positive ethos."

"I can't imagine how it would help. I am not a religious man."

"Let us discuss in the evening when I have more information. What have you to lose? A few weeks at an ashram cannot hurt. If you dislike it, come back, and we will think of something else."

Kishan Chand picked at his food in silence.

"As for work, forget about it. If you are your old self when you return, I will have a surprise ready for you."

Before going to rest, Kishan Chand sent a telegram to Manager Sahib:

> Delayed in Allahabad STOP Oversee Das business STOP Tell Munshi Ram to manage house STOP Gratefully Kishan Chand Das

# 4

## *Triveni Sangam, 1905*

The city of Kaushambi, capital of Hastinapur and renowned for justice, was ruled by the Kurus. They founded it in proximity to Triveni Sangam, the place where rivers Ganga, Yamuna, and Sarasvati—life-giving to Hindus—flow together. Over time, ashrams mushroomed along riverbanks, adding peace to its renown. Triveni Sangam endured the passage of time, though since those ancient times, the mighty Sarasvati has disappeared into Mother Earth. The city of Kaushambi, however, crumbled under assaults from invaders and later colonizers, paving the way for Allahabad—home of the British India High Court, the highest judiciary in India, since the Supreme Court stayed safely inviolate in England.

Moti Lal set up a practice in Allahabad and established a substantial reputation for saving many a princely property from being usurped by the British. He also challenged exorbitant taxation laws with equal fervor though less success. Hence, over time, he had accumulated well-wishers across a broad spectrum of society. So, when Kishan Chand needed help, securing lodgings at an ashram managed by devotees of Swami Vivekananda was well within his capabilities. The ashram followed Vedanta, the belief that every soul is a manifestation of God, and this divinity can be manifested through the yogas of work, meditation, knowledge, and devotion. That was why Moti Lal selected it. Kishan Chand agreed because zealous Sevaks enforced an ascetic, grueling daily schedule.

On check-in, Kishan Chand was assigned a room, prescribed an Ayurvedic diet, and given a midsize copper tumbler in which he was to store water overnight and drink first thing in the morning. His routine started before dawn with recitation, *Gita paath*, followed by meditation. Then came a whirlwind of physically demanding tasks: sweeping and mopping floors; serving lunch and cleaning thereafter; dusting common areas like verandas; tending to sick and elderly resident monks as and when required. This unaccustomed labor kept him fully occupied, so for evening lectures on topics like self-realization and discussions about "Who am I?" he found himself rushing to be on time. At dinner, which was light and optional, he was supposed to serve others before eating. On the first day, by nightfall, he yearned for the hard coir mattress on the floor of his spartan cubicle.

In bed, he tossed and turned, and the next morning, he was as weary as before.

On the third day, he opened his eyes to a predawn orange glow on the river. He watched the sun rise and wondered why he had not seen it before. At prayer, his body quietened; half an hour of meditation was over in five minutes. Service tired less. His stomach welcomed the spartan diet. When dusting the veranda, he heard music and realized it was the sound of rippling water. He noticed the trees, the birds, the flowers. He noticed the balmy breeze that bathed his room and that its fragrance had cleansed his heart. Thereafter, sunrise and sunsets afforded magical minutes when he padded barefoot down the steps of the ghat for a dip in the river.

On the seventh day, he slept and awoke rested, looking forward to his duties.

On the tenth day, during lunch service, when he bent to ladle *kheer* on a *pattal*—a leaf plate—he heard a voice.

"What has brought you here, young man?" The wizened fakir's eyes shone mischievously.

"Oh, nothing." This was the first time anyone had asked Kishan Chand a personal question at the ashram.

"Have you asked yourself what you want?"

"I am here because my friend forced me, and I agreed because I am a burden on everyone."

"What makes you a burden? Surely nothing physical. Your limbs appear intact. A malaise of the mind?"

"God took my beloved wife, Radha. I provided for my family, gave to charity, respected my elders. I am a good man; why me?"

"When did Radha die?"

"About a month ago. I performed all required rituals but got no closure. I am purposeless."

"Why come here then?"

"I hoped work and worship would give me answers. But I hear nothing from Him."

"He is in every breath. Let go of the past, and you will hear His plan for you. His decisions span eternity and yours a mere lifetime. So do not judge Him or others, and you will find your dharma."

"I miss her." Kishan Chand knelt to hear the old man better.

"She is at peace. If you recall her, it is for your own gratification; self-pity is greed. Thank Shiva for what you have received already. This karma means he has another purpose for you. Act with the same passionate discipline that is your essence. In action lies salvation for a *grihastha*. Prolonged anger is corrosive. Spit it out; it has served its purpose." The fakir bent his head and started eating as if the conversation never happened.

The old man's gentle aura negated the harshness of his words. As Kishan Chand moved down the line and served others, he recalled a verse in the Gita: *change is the law of the universe.* That night, he dreamt of a future where he was resolute: the earth moved through space; night followed day; every day a new beginning. True stillness comes from embracing movement—the ebb and flow of life. *To be wise is to accept change. To be enlightened is to love change.* The next day during lunch and dinner, he scanned the rows of seated swamis for the old fakir. He was not there. Or the next day; or the day after. He asked around, but no one seemed to know of him. Had he imagined the entire encounter?

Or was it Radha reincarnated as a fakir paving an alternate path? *That would be just like her.* He smiled and reexperienced their mornings in the pooja room. He inhaled her sandalwood scent; heard her laugh as she sprinkled cold Gangajal and then kissed him.

On the fourteenth day, Kishan Chand checked out of the ashram.

"As usual, *Bhai*, you were right. Two weeks at Triveni Sangam, and I feel Radha is with me again," he told Moti Lal.

He spent the next few days availing every opportunity to hold the infant—a bundle of joy with a headful of curly hair—who dimpled when her stomach was full and yawned when sleepy. She too did wonders to restore his natural optimism.

"I must get back home. I have been remiss in ignoring my newborn son—a precious gift from Radha."

"Yes, it is time. Also, I contacted my friend Bipin Chandra Pal. I invited him to visit, but he could not leave Calcutta."

"Isn't he the fiery writer and social reformer?"

"Yes. With Lala Lajpat Rai of Punjab, and Bal Gangadhar Tilak of Maharashtra, they lead the Swadeshi movement, which advocates self-reliance and revitalization of the Indian economy as the route to independence. Have you heard about it?"

"I have but tell me more."

"The first call is for rejecting all imported items, which we replace with Indian-made goods. This will rebuild the Indian economy, and that is where you come in—producing goods in India. The Bengal Partition was conceived because Lord Curzon is worried about Indians uniting, and this is his strategy—to divide us." An animated Moti Lal paced the floor and spoke with arm-waving emphasis. "Our response is the boycott movement—boycott of foreign goods and the social boycott of any Indian who uses foreign goods. Tilak says that the Swadeshi and boycott movements are two sides of one coin."

"It affects me too. Research is banned, and India is losing skill. We had the finest silks and muslins. Now, even a sewing needle must be imported. On the other hand, we keep Rolls Royce afloat. One client of mine has eleven vehicles, and elephants must pull one when it *fails to proceed,* as he says jokingly. Gandhi's loom is not only symbolic but also practical."

"Exactly. Our markets fuel the industrial revolution, leaving us behind in technical development. Strikes have already begun in Bengal and must be spread to other regions if we are to send a broader signal against the government."

"How can I help? Maybe I can take the protests to northern India—to Dehradun."

Moti Lal pulled a letter out of his pocket. "From Bipin. He says your support will be invaluable."

"The commissioner threatened to shut my business when I objected to the Partition. It is different for you. A lawyer can fight from within the system, but if I organize strikes, my family will face hardship. What else can I do?"

"Here." Moti Lal pulled out a newspaper. "Does Dehradun have a paper? News from a swadeshi perspective would help. To start, Bipin's articles from *Paardarshan* can be translated to Hindi."

Kishan Chand scanned the periodical. "I cannot read Bengali, but my friends in Dehradun will help. We will call it *Doon Patrika*." With each word, Kishan Chand became more confident. "I can start a chapter for nationalists in Dehradun."

"Great. I will send letters introducing you to the Congress Party. Later, you can meet Bipin in person."

"Agreed. And now you and Bhabhi must also agree to my request," Kishan Chand reminded Moti Lal. "Have you thought about my proposal for your daughter? I will not book a ticket to Dehradun without an answer."

"There is the question of the groom. Which son will it be?"

"Ishaan is about four and frisky as an Arab colt. He is the healthiest and brightest of all my children. And he has his mother's looks. Yes, I think he will be an excellent choice."

Moti Lal hesitated. "It is a bit sudden. Should we wait?"

"Tell me your objections, and we will resolve them."

"No, but …" Moti Lal demurred, then abruptly said, "Kishan, she is my only child."

"You will not regret this. I promise."

"Okay, but her *gauna* will be many years hence. You won't rush me?"

Gauna, the ceremony performed when a child bride is physically and emotionally mature enough to leave her parents' house, was well known to Kishan Chand.

"You have my word." Kishan Chand gave a tight hug, thinking Moti Lal's tension was normal. "I will be back in a few months for the wedding. As for gauna, you let me know; fifteen years will fly by in a wink when we are relatives."

"We will do a simple pooja then, but the gauna will be a grand affair." Looking uncharacteristically restrained, Moti Lal said,

"Kishan, remember your promise. My child is your daughter till her gauna."

"I will love her like she is my own."

"Then I agree." Moti Lal did not elaborate.

Kishan Chand boarded the Dehradun Express with a light heart. He had a baby to name, a newspaper to launch, a *sabha* to lead. And a wardrobe of homespun to purchase.

# 5

## *Dehradun, 1905–1915*

The Das family of rambunctious and sometimes disobedient boys grew with indulgence from their father but without the benefit of female tenderness in times of woe.

Not that Kishan Chand did not try.

The first month after his return from Allahabad, he requested an aged aunt to manage Radha Vilas. She left after a month. A series of widows and women from his extended family were invited to help with raising the boys and managing housework, but he found that none would stay without extracting a toll on his nerves. He compared them to Radha and thought them deficient: lacking grace in managing the household; lacking warmth in tending the children. They found him harsh and judgmental. Such was his disaffection that when he went to Allahabad to formalize his son's betrothal, he took a pundit from Dehradun to conduct rituals usually assigned to a woman.

He even tried hiring a governess.

Miss Johnson was flipping through the morning *Statesman* over a cuppa when she saw his advertisement. Relative to an undistinguished captain, having no title and not much beauty, knowing she had no chance of snagging a rich American, Miss Johnson had recently arrived in India, planning to find fortune in the form of a raja or fall in love with a dashing guardian of the Raj. *Hmm … a governess has opportunities.* Handsome remuneration and benefits, she read. Das, though not royal, seemed wealthy enough. Cantonment life had yielded only the evening gin and tonic for company, so when Miss Johnson read that Das was recently widowed, she applied.

Kishan Chand hired her with much optimism. She was instructed to give the boys English lessons, teach them manners, and ensure a dress code; they had Masterji for science and math. She was to oversee the pantry and inform Munshi Ram when food stocks ran low or if she required something special. The baby was not her responsibility.

"Feel at home," he said.

She noted the height of the pillars in the ornate veranda, the marble inlay work in the drawing room, her lavish quarters, and the lush gardens and smiled her agreement.

Primly dressed, Miss Johnson sallied forth every morning. Before beginning lessons, she called in the servants and pointed out every speck of dust in her quarters. She could not get her tongue around the boys' names: Samar became "Sam," Adrith "Seth," and Ishaan "Shawn." When the boys did not respond to their unfamiliar names, she declared it rude, so they adapted. At lunch, she demanded English cuisine, and the cook expertly boiled vegetables. At dinner, she insisted that Kishan Chand occupy the head of the table. Table manners—how to hold and use cutlery, keeping clinks to a minimum, cutting with the fork in the left-hand tines down—were enforced. One too many slices of carrot on the fork earned a patronizing smile. The boys became adept under her tutelage, but even she had no answer to the pesky problem of eating a roti, poori, or paratha without the use of hands, and the table routine evolved into a convivial combination of cutlery, crockery, and fingers.

Between mealtimes, Miss Johnson held lessons. After a while, the boys grumbled that two hours for English was too much—they had math, science, Sanskrit too—so she reduced the time. Sometimes they were too busy for English lessons, so she stocked the library and told them to read on their own. The arrangement satisfied all parties, especially since the boys aced the tests she devised. Miss Johnson was left with nothing much to do and no company for entertainment. She looked forward to dinnertime, but it was no fun if Kish, as she called him, did not join.

After a few months, trivial—imagined or real—transgressions by the staff or boys brought on the vapors, and she retired to her room. Kishan Chand bought her smelling salts, and she held them under her nose in a handkerchief. The treatment helped but not the fact that Kishan Chand nodded understandingly yet refused to reprimand his sons or the staff. Soon, the vapors grew till they became full-fledged fainting fits. One day, knowing not what else to do, Kishan Chand deployed a fistful of powdered chilies on the swooning woman, promptly restoring her faculties. He claimed the remedy worked. She said it was barbaric and departed swearing that she would see that no English woman ever set foot in his house again, though that would later turn out to be wrong.

The boys were jubilant. She had not earned their respect, and when they thought no one was looking, they imitated her accent and swinging walk, accompanied with stifled guffaws. Ishaan was particularly adept at turning pale and fluttering his eyelashes before sinking like a log.

Kishan Chand gave Munshi Ram full authority for household

decisions and increased wages for all staff. He installed tennis and badminton courts and coaches for the boys. Even baby Umang joined, carried by Samar or Adrith on one arm—a handicap worth one point—and when a toddler, piggyback by Ishaan. His first step, they told him later, was to fetch a ball and hurl it across the court. Soon enough, Umang became everyone's favorite ball boy and then an ace player. The house on East Canal Road once again came alive.

Miss Johnson's rancorous departure had a significant side effect: it precipitated a renewal of Kishan Chand's flagging political enthusiasm. A threat to his business was no excuse. Das Engineering was rebranded, and Chand became the family surname; if he were to be incarcerated and fingerprinted, repercussions would be delayed. In a few years, Samar would be old enough to run the business. Till then, if business suffered, he had properties to mortgage. *All is well.*

Boys being boys, they fought but also played together; they competed fiercely in sports and studies, but lazy summer afternoons led to a loose camaraderie that bred an intense loyalty among them. Without strict rules to follow, they became independent, self-reliant lads who made their father glow with pride.

Thus, the decade passed in tumultuous equilibrium, till one day the postal service delivered a standard blue aerogramme, and Kishan Chand's life took another turn.

# 6

## *Allahabad, 1905–1915*

Moti Lal waved one last time as the Dehradun Express steamed out of Allahabad station and then hurried home. A devastating discovery had completely swallowed the relief he felt about Kishan's remarkable rebirth. It had been a strain keeping it secret after seeing his friend filled with purpose and optimism, but he was glad he did. *The ashram corrected the course of my friend's life, but for me, it has no cure.* During a routine medical examination, the doctor had listened to his heart, detected a murmur, and declared it early onset of arrythmia. No matter how many times Moti Lal asked, the diagnosis remained unchanged.

"Change your lifestyle, Moti Lal. With a proper diet, you might live long enough to see your daughter mature into a young woman," the doctor advised.

If not for himself, for his infant daughter, he must live.

"On one condition. My wife is still weak and may not withstand the shock. My practice is young, and bad news spreads. I cannot tell Kishan because he will insist on taking my daughter to Dehradun to reduce my responsibilities. It must remain our secret."

"If you reduce your workload starting today, I agree. A happy, relaxed environment could delay the inevitable for several years. It is possible."

So, Moti Lal set out to build a routine prioritized around his precious daughter. He devoted the same meticulous attention to detail that had settled legal disputes in his favor to chores at home. His wife was recovering slowly; the childbirth had taxed her delicate constitution. At night, when the baby cried, she could not nurse, so Moti Lal shifted the cradle to his room and discovered that his off-tune lullaby inexplicably shushed the infant. He installed a goat in his back garden to supplement mother's milk. He familiarized himself with kitchen operations. When the *doodhwala* came, he inspected the cow's udders and supervised the milking process to ensure clean hands and vessels were used. After the baby was a few months old, he visited the cook daily to ensure rice, *mung daal*, carrots, and peas had been adequately mashed. He made it his business to find out every servant's name, interests, opinions, and behaviors and allocated responsibilities accordingly.

Saying he wanted to spend more time with family, Moti Lal reduced his client load. What time he spent in courts he optimized by adopting a bulldog go-for-the-gullet style of argumentation. It proved efficient, if not winning. That was all the excuse he needed to further delegate court appearances to junior lawyers. Later, years after his death, his doctor would say that it was a miracle wrought by willpower that Moti Lal lived as long as he did.

With so much change, the first six months flew by. When his wife was well enough to hold her child and handle visitors, Moti Lal sent a telegram.

> Mother daughter in good health STOP Please visit STOP Moti Lal Tiwari

Kishan Chand came with baskets of gifts and a small entourage, including his four sons: Samar, age twelve; Adrith, ten; Ishaan, four; and the newly named six-month-old Umang. His *poojari* had been instructed to keep the ceremony brief, as the groom could not be expected to sit still for long.

Pundits from both families showered blessings and legalized paperwork. The stars predict a propitious nuptial future they said and noted the moment in time in the horoscopes. The boy's name was noted as Ishaan Chand.

"Moti Lal ji, *kanya ka naam kya hai*? What is your daughter's name?" Kishan Chand's pundit asked.

"We have been calling her Ladli, but write her formal name—Leela Vati Tiwari. This a naming ceremony in addition to her marriage," Moti Lal said with characteristic expediency.

Formalities over, adults hugged while spirited children squealed and chased one another. Ishaan loved being the center of attention. His normally stern father smiled at him as if he had won a race and not stuffed his mouth with mithai. Samar and Adrith dared not tease him. Pitaji had smiled indulgently even when he had fidgeted during pooja. To the peaceful baby cradled in her mother's lap he paid scant attention, but instinctively he knew she was the reason for his royal treatment. So, he offered to hold her, but no one would allow it.

Leela cooed and smiled and stole everyone's heart.

Leela was home-schooled. Before she was five, she could read and write Hindi and Sanskrit and was starting the English alphabet. She had a flair for math, so Moti Lal's private accountant, Munshi, taught her double-entry bookkeeping, where the value from every financial transaction is entered twice. Evenings were for music and dance lessons. Her mother bestowed an exquisite aesthetic sensibility into Leela's moves.

Moti Lal tucked his daughter in bed every night, and later, Leela could not remember a time when she had not known the story of little Ganga. The telling became more elaborate over the years, and every year she understood more.

> Once upon a time, hidden from humans, high in the Himalayas, glaciers gave birth to a baby girl. They named her Ganga. She began her journey by emerging from her birthplace, called Gaumukh, and sped down the mountains, sometimes a gleeful torrent of foamy white and other times a mischievous pinging on pebbles mirrored in mountain tarns. By the time she reached the plains, she had grown into a woman: deep and calm. She enriched lives by bringing water to the crops; she enabled trade and brought prosperity to all who came to Allahabad and beyond. People began idolizing her. She became proud. When she reached Bengal and saw the vastness of ocean, she became afraid of losing her identity. She did not want to be swallowed and forgotten. So, she slowed her journey. She spread over miles and miles, refusing to go farther. Seeing her fear, the ocean quietly came inland. The two waters mingled in the Sundarbans, becoming one so that she was no longer afraid. By the time Ganga reached the Bay of Bengal, she realized she was not losing herself; she was now the ocean, and new adventures awaited. The ocean gave birth and transformed her into clouds that soared over land, dropped rain on fields to make them fertile, and eventually she

> returned home to her birthplace, where once again the mountains and frozen rivers rejuvenated her, and she was born again as the little girl called Ganga.

"Pappa, Ganga has many forms—a glacier, a river, and a cloud—but she is always water?"

"Yes. And her journey had many stages, each with a beginning and an end, but her identity is a circle with no beginning and no end. Like Ganga, our soul is eternal, though at every stage of our journey, the body experiences only some parts."

At first it was a story about a little girl that interested her. Then it was geography. She studied the atlas and wondered how faraway England seemed so big when the map showed it so small. She made an elevation map showing Mount Kailash as the highest point, with other peaks and glaciers coming to sea level. She drew the water cycle. She painted forests, fields, cities; she added birds and animals; she placed the sun and stars. She made a globe to understand day and night, and when Moti Lal pointed to England, she asked, "How did the British come all the way here to India?" That led to a study of astronomy and trade winds, and she calculated the force within a sail.

Later, in years to come, her students would ask why she started a school. Leela would say, "To foster curiosity. My father told me stories of mountains, rivers, gods, and demons, but they were also educational: history, geography, science, and philosophy. Every dip in a river, every soak in a rainstorm, every sight of a swaying stalk in paddy fields reminds me of river Ganga. Best of all, if you are curious, you will never be bored."

But with Moti Lal's urgency in raising her, there was one thing Leela completely missed: a childhood. She never experienced playground scuffles; the joy of winning or heartbreak of losing; neither competition nor camaraderie. When she spoke, it was with a poise that masked her innocence, and given her height, people mistook her for an older child.

One monsoon, Leela's mother caught malaria and took to her bed. When she died, Moti Lal's heart could not handle the blow. Frequent bouts of arrythmia made him progressively weaker. Leela, barely nine years of age, abandoned her own grief to tend her father. The doctor advised bedrest, so she took it on herself to supervise the servants and keep accounts. The doctor visited weekly and said Moti Lal had a strong will to live, so she need not fret. But he always looked sad when he said that, and one day, he asked her to leave the room while he talked with her father. After that, Pappa told her everything.

"Leela, I will not get better. Maybe six months, maybe one year—that is what the doctors say."

"You will get better, Pappa. I know it. Last night, I looked at the stars, and I saw Amma. She says she is watching over us," Leela said, not believing her own words.

"Do you remember Kishan Baoji? He is coming in a few days."

"Why is he coming?"

"I have to tell him. He is your father-in-law, and in a few months, you will go to his house in Dehradun. It is your house too. He will look after you till you are ready to be a bride. You must love and respect him."

Leela knew she was married to Ishaan, but they had not met since the ceremony, and if it was important, Pappa would have instructed her on how to behave with Ishaan, but he had said nothing. Later, Kishan Baoji too told her about his family and how much they looked forward to meeting her, mentioning Ishaan as an afterthought. It left Leela very confused, but what did it matter? Pappa looked relieved after everyone had talked.

Moti Lal thought he was shielding his little girl in sending her off as a daughter and not daughter-in-law, but it was a lapse in judgment.

# PART II
## *Leela*

Guru Ram Rai Temple, Dehradun, 1858

# 7

*Dehradun, 1915*

"This is your room, Leela." Kishan Chand flung the door open and stood aside. Leela did not move, so he gently pushed and followed her in. "Is it as big as the room in your pappa's house?"

Leela stifled sobs, covered her face with her hands, and slumped on the bed. She nodded yes even as big, salty drops flowed from her eyes to lips and chin, right through her little fingers, and fell on her lap.

Kishan Chand looked around in desperation till he spied the metal trunk stashed in a far corner. He rushed over, unlocked it, held the lid open, and noisily rummaged around.

"Look what I found." He took out a rectangular object wrapped in brown paper.

Leela continued to hiccup and cry.

Kishan Chand ripped the packaging with gusto, tossed the debris aside, and said, "See this?"

Leela lifted her head and peeked through parted fingers. She dropped her hands: her beloved pappa! She stopped crying.

Kishan Chand commended himself on a last-minute foray to Moti Lal's office. On the wall behind his massive mahogany desk, Moti Lal had hung a sizeable oil on canvas of the rani of Jhansi on horseback, wielding a sword against soldiers with guns. Clients, lawyers, and visitors to his office were seated so that the rani's horses' hoofs bore ominously at eye level, a reminder of his commitment to overturn unjust laws. Sadly, it was much too big for Leela's trunk, but on the wall opposite, Moti Lal had hung his own picture.

"Remember this?" He held up the sepia-tinted, framed photograph. "Doesn't your pappa look regal?"

Dressed in full court regalia—black damask gown, white starched cravat, and a cream-colored, gold-edged turban in place of a wig—Moti Lal looked every inch the man who defied the British and won.

"Where should we hang it?" Hearing no reply, he hammered a nail on the wall opposite the bed. "Do you like it here?"

Leela nodded.

Encouraged, he placed her mother's portrait next to Pappa's. It used to hang in Moti Lal's bedroom—taken in the style favored by families when they sought a suitable boy. Dressed in a blue brocade sari, a self-possessed young woman, around eighteen years old, sat erect on a highbacked chair and gazed serenely at the camera.

"Remember her lullabies? You refused to sleep till she came to your room and sang a *lori*."

That brought on fresh tears.

Kishan Chand emptied the trunk with renewed vigor. He placed her daily wear frocks in the drawers and formal clothes in the metal armoire. Lastly, he bent to collect the shoes.

"I can do that, Baoji." Leela sprang out of the bed, wiped tears off her cheek with the back of one hand, grabbed the shoes with the other, and deposited them in the shoe rack. "Amma said elders must not carry children's shoes."

"Well, I don't mind." He selected another photograph and faced it backward. "Will you give this to me?"

"Show me. Which one is it?"

Kishan Chand turned it around: a two-year-old, curly-haired girl held out her hands and dimpled at the camera.

"Baoji—of course." Leela stepped forward and clung to his waist. "I miss Pappa and Amma."

Kishan Chand gently kissed the top of her head. He held her till she was done crying, lifted her face, and looked into her eyes.

"I am not as sensitive as your pappa and amma, but I love you. Will you do one thing for me?"

Leela nodded.

"If anything bothers you in this house, tell me right away. Promise?"

Pappa was right to send her to Dehradun. Baoji was like Pappa, asking about her lessons, but there was no one like Amma to talk to—no one to tell her about girl problems. And what was her relationship to the boys?

Though no one told her, Leela estimated that at her marriage ceremony, she must have been six months old. She calculated that when she arrived in Dehradun, since she was eleven—same age as Umang—Samar, twenty-two; Adrith, twenty; and Ishaan, about fourteen. Samar had recently returned from college and been put in charge of Chand Engineering. Matchmakers brought proposals for Samar, but he was indifferent. Adrith attended nearby D.A.V. College, planning to follow in the footsteps of Pappa's friend Bipin.

Baoji told her to join Ishaan and Umang in home-school. Daytimes—a whirlwind of classes—flew. Evenings, after Samar and Adrith came home, everyone played games or went on walks. The boys were polite, but not knowing their role regarding this unfamiliar girl, they kept a formal distance. Baoji had not told her what to do in the evenings. What was she supposed to do? Leela yearned to be included, and it took her about a week to come up with a plan. She noted they competed in sports just as they did in studies. She started with the playground.

"How old are you?" she asked Ishaan, clearly the leader of their small brood.

"Older than you," he shot back. That was all it took for Leela to figure out how she would have the boys involve her in evening activities.

"Well, can you do this?" Leela did three quick somersaults.

Umang tried but fell.

"I can't, but," said Ishaan without trying, "can you do this?" And he picked three tennis balls and juggled them several rounds.

"No." She skipped rope till everyone got bored watching. "How long can you do this?" Then she held her breath longer than everyone else.

After exhausting her repertoire of physical showmanship, she took on scholarship.

At morning math class, she asked Masterji for a hard problem. He said, "Why is the number one hundred and eight significant?"

Next day, she showed him a drawing. "The diameter of the sun is one hundred and eight times the diameter of Earth. Sun diameter multiplied by one hundred and eight equals the distance between sun and Earth, and the diameter of the moon multiplied by one hundred and eight equals the distance between Earth and moon. Am I right?" The teacher gave her another and another till she solved problems Ishaan and Umang could not. She saw no need to tell them that Munshiji had taught her not only math but also astronomy.

After a month, she was invited to join the boys in cricket. Tall, she ran fast and became adept at fielding. Umang gave her tennis lessons. Samar and Adrith began siding with her in disputes over line calls or other clashes with Ishaan or Umang. An easy dynamic developed, and Leela experienced the innocent delights of childhood—so different from her home in Allahabad. When Kishan Chand was not traveling, he was solicitous about her welfare, but he raised her like his sons. When she climbed trees and tore her frock, it did not occur to him that girls should not do so. No cooking lessons for Leela. Like his sons, if Masterji gave a good report, she was left to her own devices.

Evenings became her favorite—identifying ferns that grew along the canal outside their house; cataloging birds hiding in gulmohar, neem, jamun, and jacaranda trees that lined Polo Field across town. The five of them often walked about a mile to Rajpur Road, where a new Rolls Royce dealership had opened. Ishaan loved to sit in the driver's seat and plan exotic trips. Excellent bakeries lined the road, and often they sat idly and indulged in a fresh toffee or cake.

One day, wandering about the house, Leela discovered the library. Books in English—Shakespeare, Dickens, Hardy, Frost—were hidden among engineering tomes and fat ledgers. Apparently, Miss Johnson's precipitous departure had afforded no time for packing books. Leela was delighted because her English was not as good as the Chand boys, and while she may never acquire Miss Johnson's diction, she could become the expert on content, and so the library became her hideaway. Years later, she would say that there was more to Miss Johnson than met the eye because she stocked the library with American authors too—not only British.

The void Leela had felt on arrival filled as she found her place in the close-knit family. She missed Pappa and Amma a little less every day. One warm summer night, she lay on her cot in the courtyard and studied the stars. As usual, she looked for Amma, but she did not appear; no star shone brighter. Ridden with guilt at losing her mother's visage, she stifled sobs, hoping no one would hear. Ishaan padded over and sat on the bed beside her. After a while, he held her until she calmed and nodded to show she was okay. Leela was too naïve to understand the emotions her arrival had wrought in Ishaan. She hugged him back. He caressed away the tears on her cheek with warm, gentle fingers. The following night, she found he had had moved his charpai next to hers. It was close enough to reach out and hold hands if she could not fall asleep.

She started calling Samar and Adrith *Bhaiya.*

"I am not your bhaiya," Ishaan said when she tried calling him brother.

"Then what are you?"

"Not your brother. Call me Ishaan."

"Okay, Ishaan. No need to get annoyed. What's the difference?"

"Big difference. You too will know soon."

Leela took to managing the house; it came naturally since she had helped Pappa after Amma died. She started keeping accounts. The family retainers sought her advice when vendors overcharged or delivered inferior goods or when the milkman (cows had been sold long ago) came late, delaying breakfast and spoiling the cook's mood. Meals were served and eaten on time; clothes were clean and pressed daily. She was friendly, capable, and genuinely interested in their well-being, so they transferred loyalty saved all these years for Radha Bibi to her.

Kishan Chand observed the change and mistakenly deduced that Leela was maturing fast.

A new vitality suffused Ishaan. His stomach tightened when he saw Leela practicing gymnastics. He told jokes to watch her laugh. He brushed her arm, in the classroom or playground, when the opportunity presented itself. He knew Leela enjoyed his company, though not in the way he did, but felt no guilt. They were married, even if she did not remember. Pitaji had to agree because his friend had asked when on his deathbed, so he had to wait, but when Leela clung to him at night, he convinced himself she longed for him in the same way. That her body hungered for him too. He would remind her when it was time. For now, it was his sweet, delicious secret.

# 8

## *Jhanda Mela, 1918*

Jhanda Mela was coming, and while everyone awaited the festivities, this year no one awaited more eagerly than Ishaan.

Held annually on the fifth day after Holi, Jhanda Mela honors the seventh Sikh guru, who escaped to Doon Valley to defy religious persecution. Guru Ram Rai held durbar, prayer meetings, in the heart of the district, and people of all faiths kept his *dera,* encampment secret. The guru's guidance inspired people of all faiths, and thus Dehradun—a dera in the *doon*—became a place of inclusion. Once a year, people of all faiths, from far corners of Punjab, Haryana, Delhi, Uttar Pradesh, and Himachal, converged in Dehradun to celebrate his vision of freedom by hoisting a towering orange-cloth-wrapped *jhanda* flag.

Locals decorated the fairgrounds with streamers and oil lamps.

Vendors erected stalls for trinkets, street food, and local crafts. Young men hawked rides and played music to attract children and the young at heart, making it a place of gaiety and commerce. On festival day, Dehradun looked like a bride draped in glittering jewels.

Three years had passed since Leela's arrival in Dehradun, and she was by now well adjusted to life with her father-in-law, his family, a steady stream of relatives who appeared and disappeared, and retainers who cooked and cleaned with minimal supervision. With a child's instinct for security, Leela, the one girl among several boys, relied on her father-in-law for guidance, and a gratified Kishan Chand did everything he could to make Leela happy. The family spent Sunday picnicking, bathing in canals, wading Sahastradhara, the shallow stream nearby, or wandering the many dry riverbeds abounding in the valley. Leela loved early-morning treks to the shrine where Shiva was said to have rested after he swallowed poison and held it in his throat to save the world from evil. Every trip was a race to the hilltop, and Leela came second after Ishaan, closely followed by the rest.

Of all the outings they went on, Leela's favorite was the trip to Jhanda Mela.

That morning, they arrived at the fairground and found it already packed. Children squealed while waiting in line for their turn at the rickety, wooden Ferris wheel cranked by a rope and pulley. Men lolled around food stalls and chatted with *halwais,* who could not fry *jalebis* and dunk them in sugar syrup fast enough to meet demand. Women in bright green and orange saris gossiped and laughed as they scrutinized fabric from cloth merchants. Sikh boys rushed about carrying flowers to the decoration venue.

Umang ran off to stand in line at the Ferris wheel. Samar and Adrith wanted to see the flag raising. Ishaan seemed undecided.

"I will stay here and keep a place for us." Umang stayed in line, refusing to move.

"Hurry. We are missing all the fun." Leela ran, wanting to see the flagpole raised.

"Ishaan, what about you?" asked Samar.

"Leela and I can stay back with Umang."

"Okay. You are responsible. Stay together, you three," he said and sprinted out of sight, followed by Adrith.

"Leela, come here," Ishaan called. He stood at a stall selling bangles, bindis, kumkum, delicate lace handkerchiefs, and other trinkets.

Leela skipped back, wondering how a shop like that caught his interest.

"Look at these, Leela." Ishaan held an assortment of glass bangles. He twirled them so they jingled and reflected a myriad of colors.

"How pretty."

"Show me your wrists."

"I have never worn glass bangles. See, mine are gold, not colorful, and they don't catch the sun like these." She spun the glass bangles, fascinated by the play of sound and light.

"First, we check for size. Let me put these on for you," Ishaan said. The shopkeeper was quick to hand him more in different styles and shades. "These will look beautiful on your wrists."

The shopkeeper had guessed right, so when Ishaan molded Leela's hands into the right shape, the bangles slid on and off easily.

"See if they fit."

Leela pointed her arms down to make them fall off, but they stayed put. She raised her hands, and they slid halfway to her elbow, and when she shook her wrists, they chimed.

"That is not how you check for fit, Leela. Here, let me show you." Ishaan held her wrists and asked, "Does it hurt when I put one on?" Leela shook her head, and he continued, "Glass bangles must be sized. They should slide on and off your wrists with the right amount of friction—enough to be comfortable to put on but not so loose as to come off once worn. If glass bangles are too big, they shatter."

Ishaan did not let go, turning her wrists, checking repeatedly.

"These are fine, Ishaan," Leela said, pulling her hands back.

"We can't have you breaking your new bangles, can we? That would be inauspicious for our first day."

"I don't need glass bangles," Leela said, suddenly wary.

"I am not giving them to you now. They are for our honeymoon."

Ishaan paid for two dozen bangles in red and green, and the shopkeeper nodded approvingly. "Right colors for love and fertility," he said and packed them in a box giftwrapped in gold foil.

"We are already married, aren't we?" Leela asked. "Why buy glass bangles for me?"

Ishaan had never felt the four-year difference in their ages as acutely as he did now; Leela did not understand the implications of a gauna ceremony.

"Didn't Pitaji tell you?"

"Baoji told me about the pooja tomorrow and that we are going on a trip after that."

Ishaan shook his head in desperation. *Typical Pitaji—no notion of how awkward it is for me to explain things.* Usually, an elder woman would be around to guide Leela but not in their house. Then he thought of Samar; the matchmakers had done their job and found him a suitable bride.

"After the pooja tomorrow, we will be married like Samar Bhaiya and Bhabhi are. You know that wing added recently to the house? You and I will both move there. For Samar Bhaiya, the marriage and gauna ceremony were done together, but since we were pledged as children, our marriage ceremony was a formal promise to have gauna when you are ready. The pooja tomorrow is your gauna ceremony."

"What about Adrith Bhaiya? He is not married, and he is older than you."

"Adrith says he will not marry. He intends to become a journalist."

"Can't we wait? Why does it have to be tomorrow?"

"Samar needs help with the business. I am going early to college so I can come back and help him. Before I leave home for so long, we should know each other. Pitaji says you are mature, and his promise to your Pappa is fulfilled."

"Yes, Baoji told me, but at that time, I did not understand." Leela looked worried, but Pappa had told her this day would come, and she was to do her duty. "We will still be friends, right?"

"We will always be friends, Leela. But tomorrow we will also be husband and wife. The trip is to help us start our new life." Leela looked nervous, so he said, "That means we will be more than friends: we will be best friends."

"Yes. We will be best friends." Leela smiled, reassured.

"I have wanted you since that first day I saw you walk into our house. I cannot wait for tomorrow. How about you?"

Leela said nothing. Umang's yell cut the tension. "Hurry, you two. What are you doing back there? It is our turn at the Ferris wheel."

Ishaan held on to Leela's wrists. "Tomorrow, I will put them on for you properly. Tomorrow night."

"Okay. I know about bangles now," Leela said and ran to the Ferris wheel.

Leela had not acted shy, or coy, or flirtatious, so he did not know how much she understood. *I kept my feelings secret, but tomorrow I can tell her.* Ishaan thought his heart would burst.

The gauna ceremony was straightforward: the pundit arrived early for the *havan* and chanted Sanskrit shlokas for about half an hour. Ishaan, in his best kurta, and Leela, in a gold-bordered red sari, sat on the floor, next to each other, heads bent, not making eye contact with anyone. Ishaan's hands cupped Leela's, and on the pundit's singsong signal of *Swaha … aah … aah*, they proffered incense *samagri* and rice puffs to the holy fire in a smooth gesture. Kishan Chand sat silently on one side, hands folded in his lap. With one last flourish, followed by a blessing, the pundit pronounced the ritual over. He gathered his pooja items and stood.

Leela glanced at Baoji, not sure what happened next. Were they supposed to stand too? Seeing the question mark in her eyes, Kishan Chand had a sudden foreboding.

"Leela, Ishaan is your husband now," he said and held his arms out to steady her faltering effort at rising. Ishaan nudged Leela as he went around the glowing embers in the *havan kund* to touch his father's feet. Leela followed his cue—daughters do not touch a father's feet—the gesture bringing home her change in status to daughter-in-law like the pooja had not. Tears dropped.

"Don't be sad, Leela. I will miss you too, but without us elders snooping around, you will see Ishaan differently." Kishan Chand turned to his son. "Ishaan, take good care of Leela." He wrapped Ishaan's palms around Leela's hands, gave a little pat, and, with eyes misting with the memory of Radha, said, "Enjoy your honeymoon. Kalsi is magical at this time of the year."

With that, Kishan Chand bustled off to see to last-minute preparations. A Rolls Royce (rented despite his reduced finances and pledge to boycott foreign goods) complete with a uniformed chauffeur had been arranged, and the cook was to provide a sumptuous picnic. A dak bungalow—cleaned, decorated, and outfitted with a *chowkidar* and maid—already awaited in Kalsi.

"I will go change into travel clothes," Leela said.

"No, don't. I will not either. Let us travel like newlyweds." Ishaan took Leela's hand and headed for the veranda and beyond to the car in the driveway.

"We have not been on a trip—the two of us—have we?"

"No," Ishaan said, holding her so close that Leela felt heat radiating through the fine silk of his kurta. He held the car door open. "This is the first of many trips—just us." Leela got in. Ishaan closed the door, jogged around, and seconds later, he was seated beside her.

The Rolls Royce hummed out of the driveway. Ishaan shifted close to Leela, put his arms around her shoulders and squeezed—his body taut in a way she had not experienced during scuffles in the playground or lessons with Masterji. She turned away to hide tears that threatened to spill and looked back.

The morning fog had lifted, bathing Baoji, Samar Bhaiya, Bhabhi, Adrith Bhaiya, Umang, and others in a golden light as they watched and waved.

# 9

*Kalsi, 1918*

The village of Kalsi is a buffer region between the fertile plains of Uttar Pradesh and the rugged Himachal mountains. It is especially picturesque in March: the hills grow green with winter rains; the sun shines warm; the rivers Yamuna and Tons overflow with snowmelt into dry riverbeds, giving birth to interconnected streams that meander in lazy curves or race as roaring rapids. It is a gateway on the historic route to Yamunotri, the source of river Yamuna, and has over time become a favorite stop for tourists and pilgrims alike.

It is about fifty kilometers from Dehradun, a comfortable driving distance.

In 1918 British India, a motorcar excursion was an uncommon experience and Leela's first. Within a few minutes of leaving the house, she was caught in the thrill of the ride. She stuck her head out the windows to feel the breeze and undid her hair, so it covered her face. Ishaan quizzed the driver about the engine and how it handled on hilly roads. Leela asked the name of every stream or settlement they passed. Conversation flowed. Before they knew it, it was time for lunch. The driver suggested a spot near a field of young *channa*.

"The farms here seem well cultivated—every corner watered by a channel," Leela said, astonished by the greenery.

"Yes." The driver laid out the picnic. "This area has been settled for a long time. Mundar and Khils have owned farms here for generations and have prospered. The Bhutias now live here too—they came from the mountains and raise sheep for wool. We have our own folk songs that we sing at festivals. Men and women dance together at harvest time." The driver pointed and sighed. "See there—my family lives on that farm. I come home when I can, but I also love to drive and must work every day of the week. Wait till we get to where your bungalow is—nature in its unspoiled splendor—different from this pastoral panorama."

Hidden from the road by majestic sal trees, the dak bungalow materialized in the evening twilight when they turned a curve, as if by the wave of a magic wand. They parked in the covered front porch. Ishaan helped Leela out of the car, and, hand in hand, they climbed the four small steps onto the veranda. The caretaker came running. He greeted them, palms pressed together in a namaste.

Leela, so energized during the drive, suddenly became nervous.

"Ishaan, what will we do here for so many days without Bhaiya, Bhabhi, Baoji, and the rest? Umang would have loved the car ride."

"I have organized a rafting trip, and we will visit Kalsi's well-preserved Ashokan edicts carved in a rock face. We will go on hikes." Ishaan kept a steady flow of trivia to ease Leela. "So many things to see, time will fly."

"But we are not here to see things, are we?"

"No, Leela. We are here for our honeymoon."

"Pappa told me that Baoji would be my father for a few years."

"Yes. Pitaji promised to delay our gauna because your Pappa asked on his deathbed. He gave his word, so I kept my feelings secret and convinced myself it was for the best because it gave you time to get to know me."

"Yes, it was for the best, because in Dehradun I was a child with no responsibilities, whereas in Allahabad, I was like an adult with no time for play."

"In that case, maybe your pappa did the right thing."

"What if I don't want to grow up, Ishaan?"

"We are growing together. It is time."

"I hope I don't disappoint you," said Leela, suddenly shy.

"That is not possible." Ishaan enveloped her in one big, warm bear hug.

"Will you be needing the car anymore today?" The driver had finished unloading the bags. "The jungles are not safe after dark."

"Yes. Come after an early breakfast tomorrow." Ishaan dismissed the driver and turned to Leela. "It is twilight, too late even for a walk. What do you think, Leela?"

"But it is too early for bed, Ishaan."

"How about you explore the bungalow while I check on dinner arrangements?" He had hoped Leela would join him, but she nodded and hurried away, her back ramrod stiff.

"Leela, I will be back soon. Wait for me in the bedroom."

Leela inspected the bungalow and made her way to the largest room, where she found the maid had stowed the valise and hung their clothes. A four-poster bed curtained with orange marigold garlands dominated the area. Cream-colored bedsheets were strewn with red rose petals and white jasmine. Leela walked around, ran her fingers over the fine, softer-than-butter silk, breathed in the fragrance, and noticed that the kerosene lamp in the alcove cast a glow that was ideal for romance, but it also created shadows to accommodate a bride on her first night.

"I have asked the cook to bring dinner to the bedroom." Ishaan entered the room and closed the door behind him. "That way, he can retire early, and we can eat when we are ready. He says he has a hot case to keep the food warm, so it must be what everyone does." He laughed, reached for the knob at the base of the lamp, and turned the wick on high. "Yes, that *divan* sofa will do perfectly. Much cozier than the icy dining room."

A flattering pale-yellow glow bathed Leela's face, softening every feature, making her skin translucent.

"At last, I can look at you the way I want." Ishaan held Leela by the shoulders at arm's length, his eyes devouring her face. "I am so tired of hiding my feelings."

Leela lowered her head, unable to return his gaze.

"My beautiful Leela. I did not allow myself to think of this night for fear of losing control." Ishaan drew her close and kissed the top of her head. He tilted her face by the chin, ran his fingers over her lips, face, and ears. "Do you know how long I have waited for you? Remember that night in the courtyard when you were crying? When I came to your bed, you hugged me and sobbed into my shoulder. I wished you would hold me tighter. After that, I wished you would cry again. Am I bad for wanting you so much?"

"After a storm, when the lights went out in our Allahabad house, it was my job to light kerosene lamps and distribute them." Leela stilled the trembling in her voice. "Pappa preferred lamps to wax candles because one lamp can last the whole night if the wick is low. I like the smell of kerosene; it reminds me of home."

"My darling, you are unique." Ishaan crushed a few jasmines between his finger and thumb and held them under her nose. "How about this?"

A knock interrupted Ishaan. He opened the door, took the food tray, murmured *shukriya*. The servant safely out of earshot, he closed the door and slid the latch.

"Remember these bangles?" Ishaan opened a familiar box. "Let me put them on for you. Come here; you will be warmer next to me." He patted a place on the divan.

"I am fine here," Leela said.

He pulled her into his lap. "I don't remember theses bangles being so beautiful. Do you? Is it the magic of lamplight or is it my heart playing tricks?"

Leela put her hand on his chest, pushing away to loosen his hold. "You are cold. See—the hair on your arms is standing."

"It is not cold, Leela. I have imagined this day a thousand times."

Frantically, Leela looked around and spotted the food tray forgotten in its corner. "Look—we haven't eaten our dinner yet."

"My poor darling. How forgetful of me." Ishaan brought the tray over to the divan. "We can share the plate." He took two quick bites and said, "There, I am done."

Leela ate slowly until she could delay no longer. She put the utensils away. Ishaan moved to the bed, gesturing her to join him. He unbuttoned his kurta and tossed it aside. Sitting on the bed behind her, he unhooked her blouse, removed the sari, and with his chest flush against her bare back, murmured years of longing into her ears. He undid the clips in her hair so they curtained his kisses.

He did not notice that she did not return his kisses.

Next morning, he looked into Leela's eyes. "I must be the luckiest man ever. And surely the happiest. And you?"

"Fine." Leela was already out of bed, sari neatly wrapped, combing her hair.

"Tell me, why were you so shy? You do not have to pretend like other brides. It is me, Ishaan. We tell each other everything. Remember?"

"I think I am not ready, Ishaan. Is that possible?"

"No. We are lucky enough to be friends already—not like other couples who see each other for the first time on their wedding night. Don't worry. Soon, you will feel the same as I do." Ishaan caressed her cheek and buried his face in her breasts.

"Everything is different," said Leela in a muffled voice. "I am frightened."

"Oh, I see. No one prepared you for tonight. Are you hurting? It is normal for women to feel discomfort. Men are different. In fact, I hear the first time can be painful." Suddenly solicitous, Ishaan said, "Sorry if I hurried you. I will be gentler tonight. But you must help me too. Tell me what you like and what you do not. By the time we leave Kalsi, I know you will wait for me as impatiently as I do for you."

For Ishaan, the trip to Kalsi was bliss.

Leela loved the days: they waded shallow streams; climbed grassy hills; hiked through sal forests. When Ishaan held out his hand to help her jump onto a high rock or ford a wide stream, she clung on like old times. They visited the pear-shaped quartz rock ten feet high, ten feet long, and eight feet wide said to be over two thousand years old. "The inscriptions in Brahmi and Prakrit scripts carry Ashoka's messages of nonviolence, along with duty, love, and responsibility toward one's community." Ishaan pointed out the writings. "Can you see the script? Do you know Ashoka's iron pillars, boulders, and shilas still exist all over India? From Kashmir to Kanyakumari, and Afghanistan to Burma. Pillars from his time have still not rusted. Even today, we can't make iron that won't rust."

At nightfall, anxiety replaced daytime camaraderie. Afraid of losing Ishaan, she agreed to his endearments, but her body held back that first night and following ones too.

Honeymoon over, Ishaan and Leela returned home and moved to their private quarters: a large bedroom with an annex furnished as a sitting room. Like other joint families, they shared the kitchen, dining, and formal room with the family.

"What is the matter, Leela? You are not yourself these days. Don't tell me you still feel shy at night."

"Give me time. I need time."

But there was no time. Ishaan was scheduled to leave for college in a few weeks. There came the day when Ishaan lost his patience.

"Leela, show me you love me. Unbutton my kurta and tear it off."

Leela stood rooted.

He tried again. "Then you show me what to do."

"I am sorry. No matter how much I try, I cannot think of you in that way."

Ishaan was too proud to beg. His father's favorite, the brightest boy in the area, and about as handsome as one could be, he was used to being eyed. Not only neighborhood girls, but even girls in the family flirted with him. What was wrong with Leela? It became a battle of wills. One day, without thinking of consequences, he said, "Have it your way. Come to me when you are ready." He delivered the ultimatum in the heat of the moment and stalked out of their bedroom to sleep in the annex.

"Don't do that. What will others say?" Leela ran after him.

"Is that what worries you? Since when do you care what people say? I will be here tomorrow. If you want me in the bedroom, you know what to do."

Leela was powerless; her body betrayed her with its own language. Could she lie to Ishaan? No. He was a friend and did not deserve deception, and he would know anyway. Leela stuffed her fists in her mouth to push back the scream building inside. She did not go to his bed in the annex the next day or the day after. Gradually, Ishaan withdrew till it was all he could do to maintain minimal decorum in front of the family. But he kept her secret. Grateful, Leela persuaded him to use the bedroom and shifted to the annex herself.

Nobody noticed their unusual sleeping arrangement, notably not Kishan Chand. He congratulated himself for having orchestrated the fine betrothal—especially when nine months later, Leela delivered a long, skinny baby with Ishaan's milk-white skin and aristocratic nose and Leela's thick black curls. By then, Ishaan was already away in college. Leela remembered his departure and how she had tried to make amends.

"I will be ready when you come back," Leela whispered and looked into his eyes. She saw fierce hostility. She silently prayed his anger would not poison his optimism—make him callous and incapable of love.

"Write to me, please." She had put a tika on Ishaan's forehead, glad that tradition forbade hugs or a display of emotion. Ishaan followed protocol and ate the mithai she put in his mouth.

"Study hard and make me proud," called Baoji as Ishaan got into the tonga and motioned *chalo* to the driver. He did not look back, and Leela knew her troubles had begun.

Then Leela found she was pregnant.

Ishaan did not come home for his daughter's birth. Kishan Chand thought it unnecessary, as it would have meant a one-year delay in graduation. He wrote, "Son, your wife and daughter are in my care. Don't worry."

His granddaughter dimpled merrily, as unaware of heartbreaks ahead as he was.

# 10

## *Dehradun, 1923*

"Ma! Ma! I'm home." Anita crossed the veranda and ran into the house. "See this? I got hundred percent marks in math. Sister Mary says I am an *exceptional* student. Do you know some girls cannot even do addition? I can recite times tables to twenty. What is *exceptional*? It must mean good because Sister Mary patted me on the head when she said it."

Called CJM by the local populace, the Convent of Jesus and Mary in Dehradun, under the watchful supervision of Jesuit nuns, had built a reputation for transforming teenage girls into well-mannered, well-schooled young ladies. It had a broad curriculum that included math and science. Originally founded in 1901 for white children, CJM now occupied spacious grounds: athletic fields, red-roofed white buildings for classrooms, playgrounds, and gardens. Explosive growth in the Doon Valley led to a growing enrollment, and the staff, in addition to European nuns, included Indian teachers of all faiths. Except for about twenty missionary children, the students were nonwhite and not Christian. When Samar enrolled his daughter Gita, Leela, recalling her own friendless childhood in Allahabad, registered Anita even though she was a year younger than the required minimum.

"Is that so?" Leela lifted her precocious child, swung her high, and lowered her into a chair. She bent on one knee and said, "Anahita, how many times have I asked you to take your shoes off before coming in?"

"Are you mad at me? You call me Anahita when you are angry."

"No, silly. I call you Anahita when I am so, so, so … proud of you."

"But I am Anita."

"Your great-grandfather was a farmer, and Anahita in Sanskrit means one who nurtures crops like Mother Earth. According to our Parsi friends, Anahita refers to their goddess of water—strong and a leader of women. For Muslims, it means pure like the surrounding air. Your dadu named you Anahita because it means something for all Indians. And that is important to him."

"And you? Do you like it?"

"I love it because you are my universe."

"But I like Anita. Sister Mary can't say Anahita."

"Anita is right for you at this age. It means innocent—like you."

Every morning, Leela combed Anita's long black hair into twin braids, doubled them, and tied them behind her ears with a broad red satin ribbon that matched her school uniform of red blouse and white tunic. Anita would shake her head to swing the braids, take her lunch box, and skip to the tonga, a horse-drawn carriage ideal for Dehradun's hilly roads. When Anita came back from school, Leela helped her wash and change out of the uniform into home clothes.

Over an afternoon snack, Anita recounted the day's happenings with much aplomb. "Amma, am I the best?"

"Not everyone is lucky enough to get Masterji's training. Dadu says if you are good at studies, you will bring honor to the family." Leela cherished her time with Anita but missed Ishaan, who was rarely home, and when he came during holidays, he spent all day helping Samar with the business. He avoided Leela's bedroom and came to kiss his daughter before bedtime. Anita, unaware of the undercurrents, idolized her father. "Like Papa."

"When can I tell Papa? I want him to be proud of me too."

"You can wait till he visits, or how about you write him a letter?"

"My handwriting is not good, and Sister Mary says I ask too many questions. Do I ask too many questions?"

"No. But do you raise your hand, asking for permission before you speak?"

"Yes. But sometimes I forget."

"In the classroom, that is the rule; otherwise, everyone will talk at the same time. Here it is just us, and I want to learn everything about your day, so you don't need to raise your hand to ask questions."

By bedtime, Anita had forgotten about writing to her father, and Leela did not remind her. If he did not reply, it would disappoint Anita. *And how can I explain that Papa's fight is with Amma and not her?*

One day, Anita came home, flung the lunch box across the room with a clatter, and marched into the main hall.

"You lied to me," she stormed. "You and Dadu are liars."

"Don't be disrespectful. What has come over you? Get your shoes off and wash your hands. Then tell me what happened."

"I hate you. I won't listen to you anymore." Anita stomped her feet. "You said we are the best, but Sister Mary said Dadu is evil.

She said he was in jail and should still be there." Anita burst into tears. "She said you would be in jail too if you did not have me to take care of."

"Shh … shh …" Leela hugged tight till the small body stopped flailing.

"Dadu wants her to go back to England," Anita sobbed. "She hates him, and now she hates me too." Anita crumpled on the floor, all the fight gone out of her. "I won't to go to school anymore."

"I am sure Sister Mary didn't mean for you to hear her. How did it happen?"

"I was walking in the hallway, and I heard her talking to someone in the classroom. She sounded so angry. I was afraid, so I ran away before she could see me."

"Your dadu is a not a criminal. Sister Mary was having a private talk with her friend. These are grown-up things we have not talked about because I wanted to wait till you are older." Leela thought of her father's decision to shield her from reality. *The world does not wait. I should know that better than anyone. Childhood is a luxury we cannot afford.*

"Why was Sister Mary angry with Dadu?"

"She enjoys teaching and is worried she might have to leave."

"Did Dadu hurt Sister Mary?"

"No. Remember what I said about always raising your hand before asking questions? I was wrong. Sometimes one must ask without permission. That is what Dadu did."

"What did he ask Sister Mary without permission?"

"Dadu has never met Sister Mary, but he questioned people who look like her. He does not say Sister Mary should leave Dehradun. Sister Mary can stay and help him by telling others who are worried."

"What is *incarceration*?" Anita persisted. "Did Dadu go to jail?"

"Yes, he did. You can drop school and continue with Masterji." *How long can I protect her from the daily unrest in the streets?* "This is not the only time you will hear things that you should not have to, and I will not have you being disrespectful."

"Well, I like recess. We play tag or hopscotch. During lunch hour, Tara, Zareen, and I share our food. I like to eat Tara's biryani, and she likes my pooris. Zareen brought something sweet. What is cake, Amma? Will I see my friends if I don't go to school?"

"That will be difficult. I can't guarantee."

"Okay. I want to go to school."

"Promise me one thing: you will tell me everything when you come home, especially if it hurts or makes you angry."

"I am sorry I made you cry."

"Tomorrow I will tell you why Dadu went to jail, but remember, he is the best. Sister Mary is too."

Anita nodded, unconvinced.

"Now cheer up. I will buy a cake for your snack tomorrow. Dehradun is famous for bakeries—not only cakes. They make pastries, rusks, biscuits, and many goodies. Now hurry and wash. I made *sooji-halwa* today."

Leela had not decided how much to tell Anita. The truth would destroy her innocence. Half-truths would make her fearful of the upcoming upheaval and ashamed of being brown, of being Indian, of being Hindu. Leela tossed and turned all night. *What can one say to a child?*

"Amma, what happened with Dadu? You said you would tell me in the morning," Anita said. "I can't stop thinking about it."

"Your tonga is already here, and you do not want to be late for school, do you? We will talk in the afternoon." Leela escorted her child out, not waiting for an answer. "I am buying a cake for snack. What flavor would you like?"

"I can't decide. You choose. Zareen brought pineapple, and I liked that."

Leela waved till the tonga was out of sight, then hurried into the bedroom. Never had she felt Ishaan's absence so acutely. In

Anita's eyes, Sister Mary was the teacher who knew more than her home-schooled mother. But Anita adored Ishaan. His word would be enough; no explanation required.

Leela rummaged through her writing desk. She opened the letter. Just as she remembered—with the queen's insignia dominant—the document charged Kishan Chand with sedition, inciting violence, and rioting. Anthropometry being more advanced in India than England, for exactly this purpose of amassing a database of seditionists in order to impose ever harsher penalties for repeat offenders, were Kishan Chand's fingerprints. At the bottom, in small, unreadable handwriting, was a date and the Punjab governor's seal.

*How am I going to tell a five-year-old about wrongful incarceration? How do I teach her not to hate, no matter the provocation?*

Sister Mary had not lied when she called Baoji a jailbird. But she had lied about everything else.

# 11

## *Amritsar, April 1919*

The years 1910 to 1930 marked a change in the social landscape of India, of which Kishan Chand's extended family was but a microcosm. An educated middle class burgeoned out of families of minor zamindars, landowners, and villagers. The government was forced to open some top-level positions reserved for Britons to Indians. Universities in Calcutta and Bombay graduated more than sixty thousand students, who entered public administration or law, making it possible for them to get organized and assert for justice with protest marches and lectures. For the first time, a resistance movement—rather than a rebellion—took hold in all parts of India till it touched everyone. From landless laborer to the middle class to princely states, a dissatisfaction with British rule fomented beneath the surface and periodically erupted into clashes against the government. It was the time when people—divided by language, state, religion, economics, and education—united in their struggle for freedom.

Their unity scared the British. The Raj dug its heels in to hang on to their crown jewel. Ever harsher penalties were imposed. Mass incarceration and lathi charges became commonplace. In the name of law and order, police excesses were justified. Indian media was muzzled. Businesses stifled. A propaganda campaign to belittle Indians and rob them of dignity was launched.

Adrith chased demonstrations and sent eye-witness reports to the underground newspapers. Ishaan kept to his studies. It left Samar to run Chand Engineering because, for Kishan Chand, what began as a sense of betrayal with Lord Curzon's 1905 order to cleave Bengal had blossomed into a single-minded obsession for self-rule. Gandhi's return to India from South Africa in 1916 increased Kishan Chand's participation in the Congress Party. He was hardly ever home.

When Kishan Chand announced he was off to Amritsar, Leela tried to stop him by using their financial situation as an excuse.

"We mortgaged our last property to raise money to meet payroll this month. You can't leave."

"Samar is managing the business. Talk to him."

"Samar Bhaiya has not been keeping well. At least one day a week, he is sick. The doctors don't know what is wrong."

"How about his college friend—the one who came here looking for work. I thought he was helping Samar."

"He spends all his time in the pooja room or kitchen. Yesterday, the cook complained about his interference. He eats special food and must add his own spices to everything. We cannot pay him, but still he stays, 'to help my friend.' Soon we won't be able to pay the staff."

"In that case, cut business costs. If Samar cannot find new business, close all satellite offices. Let that be his problem. You manage family expenses and *girvi* this house to get a loan. When Ishaan graduates, he will fix everything."

"Girvi our home?" Leela had not known the situation was so bad. "Have you mortgaged everything else?"

"Don't stop me, Leela. What good is money, this house, this business if we Indians do not have our dignity?"

"You find the most dangerous places to go to. We worry."

"I am prudent—not the impulsive sort I used to be," Kishan Chand reassured. "Another year is all we need. The British are seeing the inevitable. Did you know till 1900s they not only thought the Raj would live forever, but they also thought they were helping us—that we were too irresponsible to be worthy of freedom?"

"Take Adrith Bhaiya with you. He can write from anywhere."

"Adrith goes where trouble is already brewing. I am safer without him."

On April 13, 1919, the festival of Baisakhi brought Punjabis from far and near to celebrate with prayer and song at Jallianwala Bagh—a garden in the middle of Amritsar. Soldiers armed with .303 Lee-Enfield rifles lined up in a row to block the only exit. When Commander General Dyer shouted, "Fire!" they shot unarmed men, women, and children at point-blank range.

Shots rang out for full fifteen minutes. The screaming of injured women and children escaped the walls of the garden, mixed in with staccato gunfire. Crowds gathered outside. They deployed more soldiers to control "rioters" with whatever means available, per judicial order. Kishan Chand was in the crowd outside the garden. He was beaten with batons, rounded up, and hauled to jail, along with everyone else.

Dyer said to an all-British tribunal he had mistaken the gathering for a rebellion. They did not reprimand him and ruled that those in jail were to be detained, pending investigation.

Congress workers met with Sir Michael O'Dwyer to demand

release of the incarcerated and action against General Dyer. The governor was anything but sympathetic, but he allowed senior leaders to be released, pending identification.

"Look what he has done now!" Samar marched into the office and waved a yellow slip of paper under Leela's nose.

"What is it?" Leela expected to hear about an unpaid bill they could ignore no more. "Don't upset yourself. I can take care of it."

"Not this time. See, this." He handed her the envelope: a telegram dated April 15, 1919. Leela's hand shook as she opened it.

> In Amritsar jail STOP Come with identity papers
> STOP Kishan Chand Das

"Pitaji is so irresponsible; thinks only of himself. People are coming tomorrow to discuss a new contract. How can I go to Amritsar?"

"I am sure Baoji did not plan to go to jail. Something must have gone wrong." Leela read the telegram again. "I will take the documents, and you stay here to attend the meeting."

"You? A woman?"

"Why not?" She laughed. "If it means going on a hunger strike outside the jail, a woman might even get more attention than a man."

"I should go. He sent me the telegram."

"He addressed it to you because you are the eldest—that's all. Bhabhi can help with Anita. Yes, it is better for everyone if I go." Leela gathered some files. "Word spreads fast, and there may be repercussions here from local authorities when they hear about Baoji. Bhabhi and the children are safer with you at home."

Leela's Amritsar trip marked the first of her many skirmishes with Raj mentality. The release document required the governor's seal, which he gave as if doing her a favor; the white policeman unlocked the cell with loud oaths.

"Let us go home now," Leela said, thankful the ordeal was over. Kishan Chand had bruises and welts but no broken bones.

"They jailed us to delay holding an inquiry." Kishan Chand fumed. "Not only in faraway Britain but also in our own country, they get away with it. I am sure they will find General Dyer innocent. Even if he resigns his commission, it will be with full honors."

"How can they perpetuate injustice in the name of law and order?"

"They can because we let them."

Samar, weakened by the mystery stomach ailment, had no sympathy for his father's ordeal. "How could you do this to us, Pitaji? Do you not care how much trouble you have created?"

"What have I done wrong? I do it so you can hold your head high."

"Everyone blames me, but it is your fault." Samar had never defied his father. "Your politics has destroyed us. How can I get work when all they talk about is your conduct?"

"How dare you? Do you not know what is happening, or are you not willing to make even a small sacrifice? Did I pamper you too much, sending a cook and a valet to college with you? Where did I go wrong with you, Samar?"

"Adrith runs around inciting violence with his stories. He is the one you spoiled. I am here coping with everything, and you are complaining about me?"

"I thank my stars I did not have the money for foolishness when Ishaan was growing. We do our duty, and that is what I expect of you." Kishan Chand stalked off, leaving behind a stunned silence.

Leela ran after him.

"Samar Bhaiya is tired. Do not mind his words, Baoji. Tomorrow it will be fine."

Harsh words spoken in the heat of the moment pounded a wedge between Kishan Chand and his eldest son. Matters worsened when Samar's health deteriorated, his aggrievement grew, and he refused to apologize. In addition to financial trouble, Leela now faced family discord. She thought Samar Bhaiya was wrong, yet in the precarious position of peacemaker, she had to justify his actions.

Leela folded the paper and put it back. She could not let her daughter misunderstand Baoji like Samar Bhaiya.

When Anita came home, Leela gave her the promised cake, pulled her close, and said, "In 1919, when you were one year old, your dadu was in Amritsar prison for three days."

"Jails are for bad people. Did Dadu do bad things to Sister Mary?"

"No. Dadu asked questions of people who look like Sister Mary about what happened in Amritsar. They knew what they did was wrong, but instead of listening, they put him and many others like him in jail to keep them quiet. He is not against Sister Mary living in India."

"Then why did she say those horrible things?"

"If Sister Mary's heart is pure, she should not worry. I can talk to her."

"No. She does not know I overheard."

"Sister Mary teaches well. Respect her for that." Leela changed the subject. "Is your English as good as Papa's?"

"My English is getting better. On the playground, we talk in Hindi, but in the classroom, she makes us speak English." Anita grinned and took another piece of cake. "Soon I will be better than you, if not Papa."

"I should hope so. And cake—that is another good thing. You know why we have the best bakeries? Because so many English people live here, and they love cakes and pastries. We have learned to bake even better than them, and now we also love cake."

"Will you make it for me?"

Leela paused, wondering how to mention the subject of forbidden eggs. The family was strictly vegetarian.

"Your birthday is coming. I will make you a chocolate cake, and it will say *happy birthday, Anahita*. It will have five candles for you to blow out."

The Chand household celebrated birthdays by sending meals to the local orphanage. She would continue that but also start this new custom—eggs be damned. It was a small rule to break after what she had been through.

The British rulers, though Protestant, had allowed missionaries to promote Catholicism, force conversions, and open schools in India, as it served their purpose of promoting white superiority. Also, uprisings against overzealous missionaries gave them ammunition to fire rounds into unarmed crowds. The only way to combat slander and misinformation, Leela decided, was to start a school that treated people of all faiths equally. *What good are papers in local languages if Anita's generation, the modern intellect, was informed by English writers or translations in English? What truths would become history? Mine or Sister Mary's?*

Baoji had remodeled one wing of the house on East Canal Road into dormitory style housing for students attending nearby

D.A.V. College. Leela furnished a few vacant rooms with desks and chairs. She hired Masterji to teach neighborhood girls and boys in Hindi, math, and science. At Christmastime, she invited Sister Mary to sing carols and talk about good Christian values like justice and kindness.

# 12

*Dehradun, 1923*

Ishaan graduated with honors and accolades. Kishan Chand was happy because Ishaan would fix their failing finances. Samar was happy to have a helping hand, and Adrith was happy because Samar would now stop bugging him about the uselessness of journalism as a profession. Radha Vilas—its veranda festooned with marigold garlands and wafting an auspicious aura of sandalwood incense—looked festive like it used to in the old days. Sitar music played in the background. The cook had made Ishaan's favorite dishes.

The family, dressed in silken finery, jostled shoulders with staff, everyone lining up to be the first to glimpse his arrival. Anita wanted to go to the station, but her mother explained that Papa had written saying no one should receive him, and when Anita asked why, she laughed and said, "There are so many of us, Papa thinks there would be no room left on the platform for legitimate passengers.

"We are to wait here. Ramu will bring word when the train arrives," Leela said.

"There he is." Suddenly shy, Anita hid behind her mother.

Ramu came running, followed by the crunch of wheels on *bajri* gravel. A silver-tasseled tonga clip-clopped and halted. The horse neighed as the tongawalla pulled the reins. He jumped off with a flourish befitting his passenger. Leela, wearing Ishaan's favorite green sari with the red border and pallu, moved to the front next to her father-in-law. With both hands, she balanced the silver platter holding a diya filled with ghee, vermillion paste for tika, grains of rice, red rose petals, and fresh *motichoor laddus.*

Ishaan emerged from the rear seat of the covered carriage, looked at the gathering, and smiled. Leela's heart jumped into her throat—this man was impossibly handsome; how could she not have realized that before? Baoji stepped forward, arms extended for a hug, but Ishaan turned and reached back. His head disappeared into the canopy.

"Don't worry about the bags, Ishaan." Kishan Chand signaled Munshi Ram. "The tongawalla will get them out."

"Yes, Pitaji. I understand."

A sari-clad girl appeared into view. She negotiated the small step with Ishaan's help, their fingers interlocked in unmistakable intimacy, and together they walked the ten steps to stand near Pitaji. Ishaan folded his hands in a *namaste* and bent at the waist to touch his father's feet. She stood demurely, one step behind.

Leela lowered the platter with her left hand, the right frozen in place, vermillion paste for the tika still stuck on her thumb.

Kishan Chand leapt back.

"Wait. Who is this. Ishaan? You should tell us when bringing a guest. We must plan for a bedroom," he said, denying the obvious.

"Pitaji, this is Ayla. She is with me, so I thought advance notice was unnecessary."

Kishan Chand strode forward and slapped Ishaan, leaving a ruby-red mark on his fair complexion. "Monster! Wretch! Is this what you learned in college? To disgrace your father? To abandon your wife?"

Ishaan stood unrepentant.

"Leave my house and never show your face again." Kishan Chand bellowed for everyone to disperse and stalked off.

The crowd pressed closer together; no one left the scene. Ishaan waited till his father was out of sight and the hubbub had lessened. Then he turned to Leela and stared: a contest of wills. Finally, it was Ishaan who spoke.

"And you, Leela—what do you choose?"

Leela had been apprehensive, but such unimaginable humiliation! *Is this vengeance?*

That first night in Kalsi, it was clear they were not lovers, and after the honeymoon, he was too proud to accept duty in place of love. Still, they had made a beautiful baby. As for the woman—was she a *tawaif* for entertainment or a lover? Men overstepped decency in dance halls, but why bring her home? And why did the woman agree? And what would he say to his daughter?

Her next sentence might well decide their future; Ishaan did nothing halfway. Words failed Leela. Then Anita came running and grabbed Ishaan around the knees.

"Papa, Papa, you are here. We have been waiting and waiting. Why are you so late?"

Ishaan bent, held his daughter, and effortlessly swung her in the air a few times before setting her down. Anita's gratified giggle reached even the farthest onlooker.

"See what I brought for you." He conjured a doll from the folds of his kurta.

"So pretty. I have nothing like it." Anita jumped in excitement.

"Oh, look! When I turn it, she opens and closes her eyes." She tapped the blue irises and stroked the doll's golden hair. "She talks too. See, she laughs when I press her stomach."

"It is an English doll. Do you like it?"

"Yes, Papa. I will keep it with me even when I sleep."

Ishaan looked into his daughter's eyes, then kissed the top of her head. "I knew you would like it." Then he gave her a book. "This is called *Black Beauty*. Next year, if you do well in school, I will buy you a pony, and we will go riding." Ishaan straightened, disentangled himself from Anita's arms, and acknowledged the others as if nothing was amiss.

Leela stepped forward. "Anita, run along now. Papa will come in soon." She picked up the silver platter and slowly, deliberately refreshed the vermillion on her thumb, extended her arm, and marked a long red tika—a caress—on Ishaan's forehead. She sprinkled a few rice grains on top of his head and looked till their eyes met.

"Welcome home, Ishaan." She selected a laddoo and placed it in his mouth.

"Leela, this is Ayla."

Ayla bent as if to touch her feet, but Leela stepped back. "Do not do that," she said and summoned the maid. "Rani, show Ayla Bai in. Prepare her bath. Ayla, if you need anything, please ask Rani."

Ayla intuited the unspoken attraction between Ishaan and Leela. Unless careful, she might lose her place as unexpectedly as she had gained it. Wordlessly, she followed the maid.

Leela waited till her voice steadied. "Where will she sleep, Ishaan?"

"In my room," he said, as if it was the most normal thing in the world to bring a woman home unannounced.

Leela stood tall, proud. "In that case, Anita and I will move out. Ayla's bags will be unpacked in your chambers." As if an afterthought, said, "I can talk to Baoji, but there is no guarantee he will listen to me."

"Pitaji will do anything for you. Tell him as much or as little as you wish, but bring him around. I am staying. This is my home."

"Do you love her?" Leela asked, afraid the answer would tear her apart. *Do I blame him or myself?*

"Why do you care how I feel about Ayla?"

"I care—even if I accept Ayla, I don't understand how you could hurt Baoji like this."

"You understand nothing." Ishaan shrugged and headed in.

"Wait. If this is your home, you have responsibilities. Come to my office for your first task tomorrow."

"So, you need me now?"

"Samar Bhaiya needs you, not me." Leela twisted the end of her pallu so her bangles pealed. "I will explain tomorrow."

"Okay. See you tomorrow morning then."

Leela's spirit lifted; Ishaan had evaded her question.

"Wait. Have another laddoo. I made it myself."

"Since when do you cook?"

"I am different now—not only about cooking." She popped the sweet in her own mouth, looked him up and down, and said, "You are different too—much taller. And handsome, I might add. And you did not answer my question about Ayla."

One by one, the family wandered off. The promised drama had petered away: no tears; no fireworks. Leela and Ishaan spoke in low tones so most could not hear them. It seemed Ishaan had brought a friend home, and Baoji was getting short-tempered these days. As for Anita, she was too young for any memory of the time when her father and mother had slept together as husband and wife and thought nothing much about moving. Papa was home!

Next morning, Ishaan entered Leela's office and found her immersed in a fat ledger.

"What did Pitaji say?" he asked without preamble. Palms flat on the desk, he leaned forward till his face was a few feet away and repeated, "Have you talked to him?"

Fresh water and soap scents filled Leela's nostrils. This was not the Ishaan who had left for college. This Ishaan was a foot taller and broad shouldered, and the muslin kurta that stretched tight across his chest outlined muscle.

"A splendid morning to you too." Leela indicated the chair opposite and exhaled. "Have a seat. You will need to sit for this."

"What is this about?"

"You know that Samar Bhaiya has been unwell?"

"Yes, he tells me the doctors can find nothing wrong."

"I can tell you what's wrong—if you promise to help."

"We are talking about Samar. I'll do anything for him." Ishaan paused. "My fight is with you."

"I know, but you could have found a better way. Baoji is more hurt than I am, and he does not deserve that. Even Ayla is suffering for your obstinacy. I feel sorry for her. Fortunately, Anita is too young to understand."

"You know nothing about Ayla and me. What about Samar?"

"Do you remember Ramdev?"

Ishaan shook his head.

"Ramdev is Samar Bhaiya's college friend. He could not find a job, so Bhaiya offered him a position with us. I too thought it was a good idea, and since we couldn't afford to pay him, we invited him to stay in the house."

"You mean that man I saw at breakfast in orange robes? Looked like a swami to me."

"He is no swami and not a friend either. He is poisoning Bhaiya and hoping to take over the business."

"That is a big accusation. Are you sure?"

"I am sure. The swami robes are a ruse to get kitchen access—claims his food needs special handling. When Samar Bhaiya started getting stomach upsets, Bhabhi blamed the cook of uncleanliness. Maharaj was terribly upset; you know how particular he is about everything. He started spying on Ramdev and one day saw him adding something to Bhaiya's lunch thali—the one that goes to his office. That evening, Bhaiya had stomach cramps. Next time he saw this happen, the cook switched thalis and brought the food to me. I had some of it, and I got stomach problems. Maharaj told me he had already tested the suspected food on himself and his dog. If the cook had not gotten suspicious, Bhaiya's health would be far worse by now. It is a slow poison, and I think Ramdev still sneaks it in despite everything."

"Why haven't you thrown Ramdev out? Have you told Samar?"

"No. If I tell him, Bhaiya will ask Ramdev and take his word against ours. After Amritsar, Bhaiya vented his frustrations on Baoji, and Baoji put me in charge of the books to cut costs. Since then, Bhaiya is mentally vulnerable, and Ramdev's treachery might be the last straw. Bhabhi will not support me either. She loves Ramdev's early-morning bhajan. He sings very well—you should hear him. The kids love playing with him too."

"What can I do?"

"Talk to Samar Bhaiya."

"It is my first day back. Wouldn't it be better to wait a few weeks?"

"Ramdev is smart and suspects the cook is on to him. Plus, he asked to see our accounts, but I would not allow it. Your return will make him desperate, and he will lose no time in turning Bhaiya against you."

"I will talk to Samar. I can say we do not need Ramdev now that I am back."

"Thanks. He won't argue with you."

"No need to tell him the whole sordid story." Ishaan paused. "Betrayal of a trust can be hard to handle."

"In that case, I can tell Ramdev to pack," said Leela, suddenly all business. She pulled out a paper. "Here—sign this."

"What is it?"

"A promissory note for wages owed—to be paid when business improves. That way, Ramdev cannot come back to demand more through legal action."

"You planned all this? Since when?"

"Since the cook confirmed his suspicions, I have been keeping daily records waiting for your return. I am my father's daughter. He taught me that every mistake must extract its due payment, but after that, we carry on. We let bygones be bygones."

Ishaan signed and left, but not before he heard Leela's teasing tones. "About Ayla, have I paid my dues? Can you and I start over?"

Samar did not object to dismissing Ramdev. "We took advantage of his good nature. He stays without a salary, you know?"

"Yes. We will settle with Ramdev, I promise." The unpleasant task over, Ishaan switched topics. "Let us go over our contracts to see how I can help."

"I am so happy you didn't leave, Ishaan. Do not worry about what Pitaji says, or even Leela. They do not realize what a toll their lack of judgment has taken on me. I can barely get out of bed half the time."

"I know, Samar. Now focus on regaining your health. Soon, you and Bhabhi can go for a vacation. Leave the kids at home so you two have time for each other. How about Agra? A visit to Taj Mahal, and you will be twenty-two again." Ishaan grinned.

Samar lowered his voice to a whisper. "You keep Ayla or forget her; I do not care. Old codgers in this town have multiple wives. Why not a young man like you?"

"My priority is to get you well again."

Samar agreed with a *let us see what happens* look and took him around to meet the staff, all the while explaining he had been forced to downsize because of Pitaji's reputation. Ishaan spent the day poring over the files. Exhausted and preoccupied with the sad state of their finances, he returned home late, ate dinner, and retired to his room.

It was when he lay half-asleep in bed that he noticed something amiss. *Where was Ayla?* Her clothes were not in the closet; her valise was gone. No trace of her anywhere—as if she had never been there at all. He stepped into the corridor, but the house was quiet; everyone had disappeared into their sleeping quarters. Leela would be up, but he could not risk a trip to her room. *What might Leela think if I suddenly saunter in on her dressed in nightclothes?*

# 13

## *Dehradun, 1923–1924*

Leela went looking for Ramdev and found him lounging about the kitchen. Courteously, she presented the legally signed promissory note and said thanks. If Ramdev knew he had been outmaneuvered, he said nothing. He accepted the note with composure, saying he stayed to help poor Samar—that he looked forward to going to Rishikesh.

Buoyed by the ease of that task, Leela gathered courage for the drama sure to accompany her next move. She headed to Ishaan's chambers, where she found Ayla bathed and ready—pacing the floor, a frown on her face, eyes swollen and red, brows creased in anxiety—not even remotely the picture of a paramour who had successfully ousted the spouse in a love triangle.

Not one to beat about the bush, Leela asked, "Ayla, what do you need from Ishaan? Tell me." Hearing no reply, she persisted, "I don't know why you came, but you remind me of a trapped butterfly."

Ayla wrung her pallu, chewed her lower lip, and looked at Leela with fearful, wide eyes but revealed nothing.

"You must know that Ishaan has never mentioned you to anyone in the family by word or letter. Do you understand why we were shocked when you stepped out of the tonga, clinging to him?"

Ayla nodded.

Leela softened. "Baoji is furious with Ishaan, but I don't believe what I saw. If Ishaan wanted to marry you, he would have said so without guilt. That is how he is. So why are you here? Arriving on his arm unannounced implies a kept woman, his *rakhail*. But you look frightened, and I don't believe he would use you."

"I didn't mean to hurt anyone." Ayla heard the kindness in Leela's voice, and the tears she had held back flowed freely.

"I can help you. We cannot change yesterday, but we cannot ignore it either. Feelings will fester. Tell me, what made you come with Ishaan in a way that disgraces you? Did he force you? Men suffer no consequences; it is women who suffer their misdeeds."

Ayla clasped Leela's hands, bowed her head, and placed them on her forehead in the classic gesture of one seeking shelter. Leela acknowledge the silent plea.

"We can both save face, provided you are honest with me."

Ayla sobbed her story:

> She was fourteen and in school when her mother died. With no means of support, she had no choice but to take over her mother's singing and dancing kotha profession. That was how she met Ishaan; he had come with friends to see a performance. Unlike others, he was genuinely interested in music and arts. He never took advantage of her. One

evening after a drunken brawl among her patrons,
she begged him to stay overnight.

"You asked him," Leela lashed out in jealous rage. "Why?"

Seeing she had hit a nerve, Ayla adopted a pragmatic hold-nothing-back attitude. "Some old-time customers of my mother started making demands of me. One even threatened me. I was scared and needed protection, so I asked Ishaan for help. He stayed nights, but I did not take money from him."

"Didn't you know Ishaan was married?"

"I suspected he was—most of Ammi's clients were. Ishaan never talked about himself, so I became convinced that he came from a loveless home. Yesterday, I saw that is not true. In my desperation to escape, I did not consider how I would look to others. When I found Ishaan was leaving, I panicked. Those people would not have waited even one night." Ayla started sobbing again and hid her face in her hands. "Ishaan did not force me to come. I begged him to bring me."

Leela visualized drunken, paan-chewing, lecherous old men forcing themselves on a defenseless teen. *What right do I have to judge anyone in that situation?*

"What happens now?"

"I cannot go back to Ammi's kotha, and I cannot stay with Ishaan—he does not love me. I know that now after seeing you two. I think he took pity on me and brought me here. Living with him would be like continuing my old profession—worse, since I will not even be performing to earn my keep. Ammi planned a respectable future for me; that is what I want. But after what I did, I know it is not possible."

"There must be a way. Let me think." Leela sat on the bed. "Can you sing something classical for me?"

Ayla performed the melodic Yaman—usually the first raga taught to aspiring musicians. When asked what else she knew, Ayla sniffed. "Ammi was the finest artist in our area, and after I got back from school, she instructed me. She was proud of me."

"Do you dance as gracefully as you sing?"

"Yes."

"Okay, come with me," Leela said. "I have a solution. If you agree to the new arrangements, we will move your bags this evening before Ishaan comes back from work."

"So, what I am to do now?"

"Follow me." Leela traversed the front veranda to enter a side gate, crossed over to the adjunct wing, unlocked a room, and opened a door. "This is your room, and next door, you will teach music and dance to children. I am hiring you as the arts teacher for my school."

Amazed, Ayla nodded agreement.

"Your first student is Ishaan's daughter, and she will be here this evening at five. Tomorrow, Samar Bhaiya's daughter will join, and as the word gets out, I hope your class size will grow, and so will my school."

"Why are you so kind to me? When I saw you this morning, I thought you came to throw me out; instead, you have given me everything I wished for." Ayla looked like she might fall at Leela's feet, so Leela moved away.

"You can thank me by forgetting your past with Ishaan. To Anita and every other person who asks, you are the teacher I have hired."

"I give you my word."

"Everyone deserves a second chance, but it is more than that. You are also a good woman, Ayla."

"How do I thank Ishaan? I am grateful to him too. He saved me, and I don't want him to think I abandoned him."

"Forget about Ishaan. He has already had his fun." Leela's sarcasm was lost on girl-woman Ayla. "What you remember is that your mother loved you and wanted a respectable life for you. In her profession, the arts were put to a corrupt use, but before she died, she taught you everything you need to make her dreams come true."

"You are right." Ayla relaxed. "This place is perfect; no one can bother me here. And I promise to do my best with the students."

"Come now. Let us meet Masterji. He can teach you along with the other pupils."

# 14

## *Dehradun, 1923–1924, Jhankar Club*

Leela found Kishan Chand at his desk, writing letters.

"Do you have a few minutes to talk, Baoji?"

"Ishaan gone yet?" He spat the words, more an order than a question.

That was the opening Leela needed.

"He will leave if that is your wish. But first, hear me out. After that, if you decide you wish him to leave, he will."

With that, Leela told him about Ramdev and how only Ishaan could have saved Samar's life.

"You could have dealt with Ramdev if you had to." Kishan Chand knew Leela was right to have handled it the way she did, but he would not admit it. "Ishaan can solve some problems, but that is not enough for me to forgive your humiliation. He is unworthy of you, and he defied my principles by bringing that woman when he has a wife waiting at home."

"I thought the same way when I saw Ayla coming out of the tonga. I felt insulted. But then I thought—whatever his faults, there is not a mean bone in Ishaan's body. He may not care for convention and propriety, but he has not harmed me even when I gave him cause."

"With Ayla in his bedroom? That is not acceptable to me, even if it is to you."

"Ayla is not in his bedroom anymore. Ishaan erred in a good cause." Leela informed him of her talk with Ayla. "Please allow me to explain and then decide."

Kishan Chand listened, horrified at the extent of Ayla's misfortunes.

"Rescuing Ayla," Leela said, clinching her argument, "from the life of a *kotha-wali* was a compassionate act, irrespective of how he did it. Baoji, from that perspective, you can be proud of your son's courage. Like you, he challenged what is wrong."

"Did he have to surprise us? And arriving hand in hand, parading his relationship!"

"He had no time to inform us because Ayla gathered courage herself when desperate. Yes, he made a mistake in holding hands. Ayla told me she was nervous and clutched to steady herself. And imagine if he had asked for our permission? There would be endless debate, bringing further misery for all. Society condemns Ayla and her tribe—provides no permissible norm for their rehabilitation. What choice did Ishaan have but to bring her here?"

Baoji was even more passionate about social reform than he was about self-rule.

"Baoji, you joke that if you were to marry again, it would be to a widow. For Ishaan, bringing Ayla was something like that." Leela added details. "Till I talked to Ayla, I could not believe how cruel men who frequent dance halls can be. She was fourteen when her mother died, and she had to abandon school to support herself. Now that she has turned sixteen, their behavior was getting worse."

Baoji stayed silent, so she said, "After seeing Ayla's predicament, I find it in my heart to forgive Ishaan. Can you?"

"We cannot send Ayla back to her old life. And she cannot stay with Ishaan."

"There is a solution. I have arranged for her to move to the dormitory wing. Ayla is talented, and her mother taught her well. We will now have two teachers—Ayla for arts and Masterji for everything else."

"How about you? Aren't you hurt by his betrayal?"

"I bear some responsibility for Ishaan's misbehavior. I love Ishaan, and now that I have woken, I will make amends. I want him to stay here as my husband and Anita's father." Leela did not elaborate on the fiasco her marriage had become during Ishaan's college days. Instead, she described Anita's joy at having Papa home and about how difficult it was to raise a child alone.

"Leela, if you are sure, he can stay."

"One last request: I am not ready to move to Ishaan's chambers yet. Can Anita and I continue staying in the main house?"

Leela was at her desk shuffling papers when Ishaan strode in.

"We need to talk." His tone was formal, serious.

"If it is about Ayla, she moved. If it is about Ramdev, he left last night for Rishikesh." Leela kept her tone light, friendly, relaxed. "He seemed reluctant to meet you. Maybe because he saw all that drama you created on arrival."

Unfazed, Ishaan eased into a chair and made himself comfortable.

"What did Samar Bhaiya say?" Leela asked.

"Samar knew Ramdev was no asset in the office. He agreed, and he eagerly moved on to business. That is what I need to talk about; one day is enough to see that Pitaji and Samar have sold or mortgaged most of our properties along East Canal Road. I asked Samar why he does not care. He says Pitaji put you in charge of finances. How are you paying the bills?"

"Well, we have the farm in Majhra; we still grow our famous Basmati."

"That is not income."

"Baoji gave the farm on a *theka*, lease, to the family who used to look after the cows when he remodeled the house to create student housing. He also gave them the horses and carriage and asked the syce to help them. They live on the farm and give us rice, wheat, mangoes, seasonal vegetables, fruits—enough for our needs. Baoji does not ask them for money—their taxes are high enough—especially now that he has hidden a printing press in their cowshed. He even spends nights there when he is working on a release."

"So how do you pay the bills?" Ishaan persisted.

"Thanks to that arrangement, we have food. We have less staff, fewer expenses. We manage. I have not paid the cook and some others, but they are old-timers and so loyal to Baoji they will not leave. I keep a separate account for household expenses and tote their wages as backpay. See here." Leela held out a big, bulky ledger and rattled numbers.

"Your glass bangles—are they the ones I bought at the mela?" Ishaan was not listening anymore, his eyes transfixed on her wrists.

"Yes. I have worn them since the first night you put them on." Leela slid the heavy book across the desk. "Here—look at this."

Ishaan looked: green and red glass bangles encircled delicate wrists, unbracketed by traditional gold *kada*-style bracelets. No diamond ring on her finger or studs in her earlobes; no gold chain around her neck.

"You hocked your jewelry, didn't you?" he barked, not knowing why he reacted that way.

"Not hocked. I sold it." Leela was unperturbed. "I don't need it, and they pay more if you sell." She stroked the simple black beads of a traditional *mangalsutra* worn by married women and said, "I have all the jewelry I need."

"Now that I think of it, you did not have much to sell. Your father did not give because you were a child when he died, and later, knowing Pitaji, he probably forgot. What did you do? Do we have a loan against this house as well?"

"You didn't miss anything. This house is more than brick and mortar. It has kept our family together; it is our home."

"Then how?"

"Umang sends money from England when he can—saves it from his scholarship. I think he does odd jobs, though he has not said so. He writes long letters to me because we cannot afford a ticket for a visit home. He will return after he graduates."

"Umang knows about our money problems, and I don't?" Ishaan was livid. Leela shrugged and reminded him that Umang was home when Baoji made her responsible for the family finances and Ishaan was in college.

"Still, that can't be enough to support this household. Tell me what you are up to. I will stay here till you do."

"Do you really wish to find out? Like your father, I believe all is well now that you are home. Isn't that enough for you?"

"You can tell me. I can handle whatever it is you are hiding."

"It's a long story, and Baoji knows only some parts. If I tell you, it must remain between us."

"I can't agree without knowing."

"It was Pappa's wish. The story goes all the way back to our wedding day when I was six months old and you four years."

"I can keep a secret as well as you."

"During that week we got married and Baoji stayed at Vivekananda Ashram, Pappa was diagnosed with a heart murmur. When Baoji returned from the ashram, he was a recovered man, and Pappa did not tell him about it because he feared the bad news risked a relapse."

"I would probably do the same."

"Instead, Pappa introduced Baoji to his friends in the Swadeshi movement. Later, Pappa's health got worse, but there was never a good time."

"All those years, Pitaji did not know?"

"Pappa made his doctor keep it secret from everyone, and Pappa prepared me for the inevitable with rigorous schooling. There was no time for play, and I had no friends my age till I came to Dehradun."

"Did he mention it to your mother?"

"Amma was always delicate. He delayed telling her too. He had me sit with Munshi ji, his bookkeeper, from the beginning because he wished me to relieve Amma from her responsibilities once he was gone. But then Amma died before him."

"When did he inform you about his health?"

"After the doctors gave him a year to live. Baoji brought me with one trunk—some clothes, family pictures, and books. One day I was looking in the home vault for something to sell and found bank papers. It's not much—he stopped practicing per the doctor's advice—but it's everything he had."

"But you were a child yourself. So much responsibility ..."

"My life was reversed: a grown-up when I was a child in Allahabad and a child in Dehradun when I should have been a grown-up. My excuse is that it was the first time I had no responsibilities.

"Why didn't he tell Pitaji when he went to fetch you?" Ishaan asked.

"Because Pappa put his money in our names—yours and mine. Baoji's responsibility was to raise me like his daughter for the first few years. Pappa worried Baoji would think it was a dowry and refuse to accept. That first day, when Baoji showed me my room, he unpacked for me: clothes stashed into the armoire, pictures hung, and what looked useless, like Amma's jewelry and papers, he put into the safe. I sobbed the whole time."

"Does Pitaji know now?"

"No one knows about any of this."

"How long before your money runs out?"

"Our money. You have time. Bhaiya trusts you; otherwise he would not have agreed to dismissing Ramdev. He will not allow Pitaji into his office—not that Pitaji wants to—but with you, it will be different. I know. You can get us back on our feet soon."

That night as Ishaan was getting ready for bed, he realized he had again forgotten to question Ayla's disappearance—and that instead of remorse, he felt relief.

Leela had waited all day for Ishaan to ask for Ayla's whereabouts.

That Ishaan forgot or chose not to ask made Leela hit the bed, humming under her breath, tingling with optimism.

Over the years when Dehradun became famous for a world-renowned Sarod player, Kathak and Bharatanatyam dancers, and several classical singers, Leela would cite Ayla's arrival as the catalyst. Leela and Ishaan launched the Jhankar Club, a venue to host an annual music and dance festival. Performers from all over India congregated, attracted by their hospitality and sponsorship. Connoisseurs credited the Chand family for revitalizing classical art forms dying in British India. Few remembered, if they ever knew, that it started with an act of defiance that almost ruined the family.

Neighbors said Leela had been lucky to find a teacher as talented as Ayla Bai. A few relatives complained about the unconventional arrangement in the beginning, but the extended family dismissed them as old-fashioned, especially Bhabhi and Samar—the elders. No one dared to bring it up with Baoji. Without fuel, gossip died a natural death. The household staff, loyal to Leela, took their cue from her and showed every courtesy to Ayla like they did to Masterji.

Kishan Chand periodically voiced concerns, but as the dreadful day dimmed in his memory, he forgave Ishaan and admired how he had gained Samar's trust—an exercise where he himself had failed—but not enough to ask. Best of all, Samar's health improved so much that he started talking about getting a new job. No one missed Ramdev, including Samar.

As for Leela, every fiber in her body came alive and burned with unspent energy when she thought of Ishaan. She looked forward to tasks they did together, but time without him dragged. If only she could figure out how to devise a trip to Kalsi … the outcome would be different.

# PART III
## *Ishaan*

British camp. Troops encamped at the entrance to the Keree Pass, north of Meerut, about eighty miles distant of Delhi. Engraving from 1858. Engraver unknown. Photo by D Walker.

# 15

*Garhi, 1923*

Ishaan was excited to be back in the fray. He spent a week tallying records, going back in time since the inception of Das Engineering. There was no doubt about it. Leela was right. After Samar started managing, business had declined precipitously. Samar leveraged Pitaji's reputation for quality to bid high, then failed to deliver even on minor projects, let alone big ones that made the company legendary. Samar deserved the rejections he had received on new bids.

Yet his heart would not blame Samar.

All the aggression in the family had gone to him and Adrith. Samar avoided conflict. Not that he was afraid. As children, when they fought, Samar would throw his lanky frame in the middle of their two muscular bodies to block punches—never spoke a harsh word or took sides. When Amma died and Pitaji fled from fatherly duties, it was Samar who kept them together; he shelved his own grief to rock Umang, tell bedtime stories, and sing lullabies. In favorable times, he was a role model to them, but his refusal to acknowledge the ugliness of the empire had left him unprepared for battle. It must have taken a lot out of him to have to face Pitaji's stubbornness in the face of financial ruin. And as for Ramdev's treachery—thank heavens for Leela—good, he did not find out.

Ishaan decided to direct his energy to gaining new business. He visited Pitaji's old clients.

"Mr. Kishan Chand Das? We hear your father does not even go to work—wearing homespun and all that. Changed the company name, hasn't he? How do we know we can trust your new management to get the work done?"

Then he called on Samar's recent clients.

"We hear complaints about the quality of work by Chand Engineering. Not what you guys used to be, eh?"

Everyone found a reason to disparage the company. One more week of rebuffs, and Ishaan accepted that he was wasting precious time chasing old avenues while Leela's bank balance dwindled daily. Then one day, Ishaan found a whiskey bottle stashed behind some bulky books. *That explains Samar's afternoon naps.* It would not help to confront him; he would be defensive. Ishaan placed the bottle back and arranged the books as before. Now he knew that Chand Engineering was dead. And worse, it was not only money, but the family reputation was also at stake. He had to build a new company.

How did Pitaji grow his business so rapidly? He too came to Dehradun penniless, and the colonists were as powerful then as now. How did he do it?

Dehradun needed water, and Pitaji built canals, long ones with ingenious designs. Kalapathar, Jakhan, and East Canal had outlets at intervals to provide drinking water for horses, people, and irrigation too. They supported community enterprises: pools for dhobi-ghats; water channels to operate small flour mills. On family picnics to their farm, Pitaji waved proudly at the green paddy fields, saying, "Our basmati rice is the best because my canals bring pure Himalayan water here." Rajpur Canal flowed along wide, tree-lined avenues and eventually filled the pond near Jhanda Mela grounds—*the place where I bought Leela bangles.*

The next day during his usual morning jog to the parade grounds close to East Canal Road, watching the Gurkha regiment practice bayonet charge against straw dummies, shouting, "Hai," Ishaan noted how every inch of the field had fierce activity in progress. Trainees overcrowded the bayonet charge till it looked like they were in danger of slashing one another into ribbons in addition to the straw-stuffed life-size targets. But the boys—with sturdy legs, ropy arms, and expressionless faces betraying no ambivalence about the mayhem their action would cause in battle—were accurate in their aim. *Hai. Hai.* A single forceful jab that would have spilled a man's guts made such a clean cut in the burlap that not a single straw spattered out of the dummy. Charge. Stab. *Hai. Hai.* Return. Repeat.

The British successfully deployed over one million Indian troops overseas to fight the Great War. Some estimated that more than sixty thousand died, and an equal number were wounded. The British Indian Army was growing because in addition to fighting in Europe, many divisions remained in India for internal security, guarding its borders, and for training new recruits. In 1913, the Dehradun Cantonment Board was created to handle logistics of military expansion. A new cantonment was under construction on the other side of town.

Dehradun was growing even faster now than in Pitaji's time.

Military expansion required not only water and food but also barracks, clothing, equipment, parade grounds, and practice fields. The British gave contracts to Indian merchants who haggled with farmers and vendors for the lowest price but treated them with supercilious tightfistedness. This resulted in shortages and problems with morale. If, like Pitaji, he was to establish a reputation for reliability and quality, clients would come to him. Dehradun was on the way to becoming a military showplace—the best-trained, best-fed, best-dressed, best-housed Indian officers would be proud to call it home—and he would make it happen. He may start as a lowly peddler, but the Chands would be industrialists.

The staccato sounds of the bayonet charge continued as he ran back. At the office, he pulled out one file after another till he found the one labelled PWRIMC. Hidden among progress reports and invoices, he found the gold-embossed invitation card:

> Prince of Wales Royal Indian Military College invites you to its inauguration on March 13, 1922, by his Royal Highness, Prince Edward VIII, the Prince of Wales.

The blank space was filled in with blue cursive script: *Mr. and Mrs. Samar Chand.*

A training institute had been built on the old Rajwada Camp, one hundred and forty lush acres adjacent to the Garhi village, so Indians could hold positions in the officer cadre. No doubt it was Pitaji and his friends who forced the British hand. The Prince of Wales Royal Indian Military College, or PWRIMC, was a school for training Indian boys with British public-school style education prior to attendance at the Royal Military Academy, Sandhurst. Lord Rawlinson had headed a committee that recommended that an institution to turn Indians into British officers was beneficial to the empire, as it would strengthen their ability to fight world wars and create a foothold in Asia against China and Japan.

The Prince of Wales himself came to grace the opening ceremony, but there was no evidence that Samar had attended. That seemed in character. His contract was for building the playing fields, and he avoided the British. The school had recently hired groundskeepers, but their company was still responsible if major problems arose—so far none, thankfully.

Ishaan made notes: Lt. Col. H.L. Houghton of the Sikh Regiment took charge on February 22, 1922. The mess contractors were M. S. Hazir and Co. and the mess staff mostly Goans. JGC Scott—a civilian—was the headmaster. British and Indian masters made up the staff.

Ishaan wracked his brain. Where did Indians have an upper hand in military training? He visualized the Royal Military College commemorative pageantry: marching bands; eyes-right salute to the distant queen. And glorious horsemanship—even the smallest raja, maharaja, or nawab maintained prized stables. Who could help him? Then he remembered: Ravi, closer in age to Samar but a competitor in sports, best friend, and his counsellor since childhood. Excited, he dispatched a telegram:

Arriving tomorrow STOP One-week visit STOP Ishaan

Major Ravindra Rathore had survived the Great War unmutilated and earned a promotion—rare for an Indian—to become an officer. Upon returning home, he had reenergized the listless Meerut Imperial Riding and Polo Club with enthusiasm and expert coaching. Ravi was a born horseman and of royal lineage to boot. He organized gymkhana days and competitions where cavalry regiments of the British and the British Indian Army fielded teams in exhibition matches—invitations were much sought after—making Ravi and the Meerut Polo Club proud. He was delighted to see Ishaan.

"What brings you to Meerut, my friend? Do not tell me you have reconsidered my offer to join our team? From what I remember, you took to polo as if you had been riding since childhood."

"Only because I had the best coach." Ishaan grinned. "I haven't ridden lately but wouldn't mind a few chukkers. See if I can stay in the saddle and wield a mallet at the same time."

"You were a natural; your father kept horses. Whatever happened to them?"

"Two—we had two horses, and not spirited Arabs or anything like what you had. I never rode as well as my father. And you? When did you begin riding?"

"I was riding Father's horses from an early age. At three, I was in a saddle with Baapji. At five, I was riding my own pony on the racecourses. By thirteen, I was galloping bodyguard horses in the cavalry, sometimes bareback! Yes, I was thrown many times, but that is a mandatory coming-of-age ritual."

Over dinner, Ravi recounted some wartime stories, and Ishaan his athletic achievements. Ravi was still a bachelor; "Polo is all the passion I can handle," he said.

"Tell me, why are you here, Ishaan? Sportsmanship aside, something else is on your mind."

"You are right." Ishaan did not know where Ravi's loyalties lay, but he had to be truthful about his father's activism. He laid the groundwork:

"My father married his childhood sweetheart—my mother—and built a successful engineering business in a short time. The Bengal Partition announced in 1905 disillusioned him about his British partners when they scoffed at his requests to roll it back. Around the same time, my mother unexpectedly died, and my father felt he had lost everything. I was four, and my brothers were still studying. Munshi Ram, his personal manservant, worried he would go mad or kill himself or do something drastic. Fortunately, his friend—my father-in-law—came to the rescue. He sent Pitaji to an ashram to rejuvenate. He recovered but in protest joined the self-rule movement. So now our community lauds Pitaji, but the British term him traitor. Samar, my elder brother, is of indifferent health and cannot run the business. Adrith, my second brother, is a journalist—he says he must balance the biased reporting by the likes of the *Stateman* and BBC by telling the Indian side of the story. He runs the paper Pitaji started when he is not courting arrest. Umang is still a student."

"How about your wife? I seem to remember a mischievous girl with dimples you used to be crazy about."

"Leela kept the family together during my absence," Ishaan said formally. "Now it is my turn to pitch in."

"But I am a military man. What do I know of business?"

"I thought if I could pick your brain, bounce ideas, we might think of something."

"Let us start tomorrow, and we must find a way to have some fun. You know, all work makes Johnny a dull boy …" Ravi looked at the wall clock. "And you must be tired after the journey."

"Before we call it a night, about all those medals on the mantelpiece, how bad was it really? Weren't you in Germany? Or France?"

Ravi stood, saluted, clicked heels, and sang in menacing bass:

> Johnny, get your gun, get your gun, get your gun.
> Take it on the run, on the run, on the run.
> Hear them calling you and me,
> Every Son of Liberty …

"Enough. Enough." Ishaan laughed. "It seems you need rest more than I do."

"Your room should be ready. Ring the bell if you need anything, and my man will be there."

Ishaan switched on his best British accent. "Usually I sleep like a log, old chap, but will be sure to let you know if arrangements don't cut the mustard."

"You devil." His good humor restored, Ravi led the way to the bedrooms. "Do you remember that summer I taught you polo? My sister couldn't keep her eyes off you."

# 16

*Meerut, 1923*

Per cantonment cuisine, breakfast was typically English. Both friends dug into hearty porridge, sausage and scrambled eggs, and thick slices of toasted bread topped with butter and marmalade. Both polished off sizable helpings before tackling the teapot.

"How do you stay trim?" Ishaan asked. "If I ate like this, I would be round."

"It's the military—no rest for the weary and all that, you know."

"And no peace for the wicked." Ishaan daubed his face with the napkin. "Talking about wicked, the British love Dehradun, so where we had farms and forests before, we now have cantonments and training camps."

"What do you mean?"

"You know what goes on in their heads. Explain it to me."

"Now that the Raj has moved its capital from Calcutta to Delhi, they have an expanded interest in our northern mountain areas, and the military faces new challenges. For example, the Army Remount Depot's prime function was to supply quality horses. The system barely worked on a small scale before but broke completely during the war-expansion effort in India. The stallions and mares are ridden by sowars, and riders and demand exceeded supply. The price, set by the government, that could be paid per horse is too high. Regimental purchasing officers are left with the most inferior animals." Ravi was warming up. "Also, for hilly areas, they need mules for mountain transport of arms and munitions, and it means greater demand for stallions, for breeding."

"Admit it: from the horses' point of view, it is an idyllic life—being fed and exercised in a variety of ways, not least with the fleet of donkeys at hand. But I can think of some practical difficulties." Ishaan grinned. "I bet the donkeys don't give a damn about those snooty Arabs you love so much."

"Funny. My uncle is researching artificial insemination. Another problem with the new style of warfare with guns and cannons is that it makes the horses skittish. I am training horses here to handle this, and through the Saharanpur Depot, we are supplying Dehradun, though they always act dissatisfied. I hire runners for the job."

"I can be the go-to dealer for the military: uniforms, food, artillery, construction, and horses—especially horses. We can have polo matches in Dehradun."

"Yes, we can't be wearing khadi in battle. But I do my bit for the country too."

"Like my father?"

"Yes. We have a love-hate relationship with the British. We admire their regimen and military skills even as we condemn the colonial occupation. Your father must continue his struggle as I continue mine."

"You two fight from different angles," said Ishaan, pleasantly surprised and relieved he would not have to defend his father.

"The British have a history of divide and rule. Long before the Bengal Partition, they imposed brutal land taxes that drove farmers into impoverishment. Soldiers fought for independence alongside farmers, so they called it a *mutiny* and deployed more military. The fight lasted about eighteen months. It shook them out of complacency, and after that, regiments were reorganized along language and regional lines, such as the Sikhs and Gurkhas. The strategy worked."

"That must be how Dyer could order Gurkha soldiers to fire on the Punjabis and get away with it. And Sikh soldiers are deployed in Bengal."

"Muslims cannot be distinguished by language or region, as they are in all states, so the Bengal Partition."

"Hence Pitaji's objections!"

"They marginalized us too. Eighteen seventy-seven was a watershed year when royal families were offered 'protection,' and with much pomp and pageantry, the British decreed us 'aligned.' So, here I am—an Indian fighting British wars."

"And we have no say in the matter," agreed Ishaan. "Pratap Singh, the aristocrat of Jodhpur Lancers, was seventy-three years old when he fought in the Great War. British royalty was happy to wine and dine with him, but when he asked for representation for India at the Paris Peace Conference, they denied his appeal. We did not get a seat at the table."

"It is not all bad. I am accorded respect—in our microcosm—Indians and British are equal; and I get to ride horses and play polo." Ravi changed the subject. "My life is good."

"Didn't you have an uncle who bought a Rolls Royce every year? He had elephants pull them around because the bloody things never ran."

"Ishaan, your initiative to industrialize India is as important as your father's activism."

"The Prince of Wales Academy in Dehradun was founded to satisfy Congress's demands for appointing Indian officers."

"Allan Hume, a Briton, helped the resistance in Calcutta," Ravi said. "Some must agitate for self-rule, some like me must learn their military skills, and some like you must rebuild the economy."

"Napoleon said an army marches on its stomach, and his army was the first to use canned foods. I will make sure Indian soldiers are as well fed and kitted as any Brit."

"We do have a wonderful mess." Ravi patted his flat stomach.

"Meerut is one of the oldest and largest cantonments and funnels munitions, food, and clothing to neighboring bases. If I find contacts in Meerut, I could supply growing demands in Dehradun. Could that be a start?"

"Brilliant. Tonight, we will go to the club, and you can charm everyone with your elegance. Tomorrow at the Gymkhana, you can wow them with your athleticism. Do you have a suit by any chance?"

"I brought a suit, but I refuse to dance."

"Not regulation. You loll around and look bored. I do not know how you do it; in a trice, the pretty ones will gravitate to you. But don't get distracted—it's work, and that's an order!" Ravi looked stern. "Fortunately for me, English women who need a dose of titillation from time to time are attracted by my horse-riding prowess, and I am seldom alone."

Ishaan had given himself a week in Meerut. In two days, he not only collected business cards, but at the Gymkhana, he resurrected his riding skills—enough to earn backslaps from men and swoons from women.

# 17

*Dehradun, 1923–1930*

A fragrance wafted into Leela's office. Cologne? She put the pen down and looked. A tall, well-built man briefly darkened the doorway before stepping in. He wore an expensive light gray suit. Chocolate-brown eyes below the distinctive broad forehead sparkled at her.

"Ishaan? I did not recognize you. We were not expecting you for another two days."

"My work in Meerut was done. I wanted to stay longer and brush my horse-riding skills, but duty calls." Ishaan was as excited as Leela had ever seen him.

"No one told me you were back."

"I arrived late last night, and I let myself in. Ravi sends his regards to you. He admired Pappa, you know."

"Have I met Ravi? I don't remember."

"It was a while back, but you sure made an impression because he remembers you." Ishaan turned to leave. "I have a client meeting tonight, so don't wait for dinner."

"And here I thought you hurried back for me." She smiled to match his exuberance and tilted her neck for a better look. "Why the suit?"

"Well?" He opened his arms wide and struck a pose. "Do you approve?"

"I can't say without a proper inspection." Leela walked around the desk until she stood a foot away.

"Hmm. No tie?" She eyed his bare throat: above the open starched collar poked a tiny Adam's apple. *Why do I want to touch it now?*

"Ties are too formal," Ishaan said.

Leela raised her hand, palms open, itching to caress his bare skin, but instead pointed at his forehead and said, "That lock of hair—push it back," and with great deliberation, slowly stroked it away.

"Did you know I play polo?" Ishaan asked.

Leela shook her head.

"Ravi taught me one summer. It might be our ticket to solvency; the army loves to field polo teams."

"I remember the polo field in Cantt. Great place for birdwatching." Leela sensed polo talk was a diversion. "What is in the shoulder bag? The leather is stretched so tight it looks too bulky for papers."

"Not now. Maybe later."

"I await—with bated breath." Leela did what she had imagined since he walked in the door. She caressed his Adam's apple. True, Ishaan had not responded to her touch, but he had not stepped back when he saw her approach. She allowed herself to revel in a newfound feeling of an age-old desire.

"You are right. No tie." She sighed.

At lunch, the cook told her Ishaan had asked him for *navratan* pulao and also some uncooked basmati rice from the farm.

It did not take long for the new routine to settle in.

Starting with a contract from RIMC for basmati, Ishaan broadened the business. He set up manufacturing plants: condensed milk and baked beans; breweries and bakeries; uniforms. His stables were sought after. Because RIMC produced such valorous soldiers, in 1932, the Armed Forces Academy was established with the first class comprising forty recruits who were trained in a variety of sports, adventure activities, physical training, drills, weapons training, and leadership. Future military leaders of the Indian Army had character enshrined in their warrior code and motto: *veerta aur vivek*, valor and wisdom. Dehradun became home to military legends. At independence, India's first field marshal, Sam Manekshaw, was one of these inaugural cadets.

Ishaan paid off property loans. Leela cleared the wages backlog and upgraded her school desks and chairs. Samar became a science teacher; he gave up alcohol and apologized to Kishan Chand, who acknowledged that business required a resilience his gentle soul did not have. Relatives once again started sending children to attend nearby schools and were boarded at home. Radha Vilas was repaired for leaky roofs and crumbling walls. It glowed again with fresh *putai*, a chalk solution equivalent to paint. Terra-cotta pots—painted an earthy red with *geru* and planted with fragrant chameli—lined the driveway. Gardeners tended mango, papaya, and lichi groves with diligence. Family and friends competed on the tennis courts and filled sunsets with laughter.

Ishaan often stayed late at work—business, he said. Leela knew it was a convenient lie; he was now much sought after by clubs and colleges in Dehradun for his sportsmanship: cricket, tennis, steeplechase, showjumping, and even polo. More worrisome, he was a fixture at the Cantonment Club favored by the British, even spending nights there after a match followed by celebratory drinks.

Anita juggled school, sports, music, and dance lessons and came home only to grab a bite.

"I am going," Anita called. "It's time for my class with Ayla Didi."

"Already? You just came."

"Amma, I finished my homework. Masterji said I solve math problems even faster now. And you know Ayla Didi makes sweets for me, so I don't need a snack."

"Don't stay late—you have to rise early for school." What else could she do? She was the one who hired Ayla when she could have easily sent her packing. *I owe her: Ayla filled a vacuum in Ishaan's heart that would otherwise have stored poison.*

After dinner, Leela would get back to her desk: weekly letters to Kishan Chand and Adrith were upbeat and newsy, giving accounts, lauding births, grieving of deaths, and offering help if needed in whichever town they happened to be. She talked little about herself, Anita, Ishaan, or Ayla since there was nothing new to say. To Umang, she wrote her school was growing now and to come back soon; their money troubles were in the past.

A few times, Leela had gone to see Ishaan's matches and joined him at the club. The looks, laughter, and soft touches of scantily clad women flirting openly with Ishaan, even as he introduced her to them, haunted her when she lay lonesome in her bed. She ached herself to sleep. *Was it how he once ached for her*?

She could go to him, but what if he dismissed her? Or worse, pretended like she once did?

# 18

## *Dharasana Salt Works, 1930*

The Dandi march, Gandhi's first civil disobedience satyagraha, was designed to awaken citizens to the economic hardships caused by British laws, specifically the salt tax, as it affected everyone. On March 12, 1930, he set out on foot on a twenty-four-day, 240-mile journey from Sabarmati Ashram in Ahmadabad to the seaside town of Dandi, accompanied by a few volunteers. After each day's march, the group stopped in a different village along the route, and Gandhi ji explained how the tax on fundamentals like salt was especially cruel to the poor and landless. By the time he reached the Arabian Sea, hundreds had joined the march. On the morning of April 6, Gandhi and other satyagrahis picked up handfuls of salt along the shore, thus "producing" salt and breaking the law. Not arrested yet, Gandhi continued southward along the coast, making salt and addressing meetings. Every morning, Leela read accounts of the march, including Adrith Bhaiya's, who had been following Gandhi around for months now. She was putting away the papers when Kishan Chand strode in.

"I am leaving today to join the march, Leela."

The satyagraha at Dharasana was scheduled for May 12. By now, mass civil disobedience had spread throughout India as millions broke the law by making or buying illegal salt. Even the *Statesman*, the official government newspaper that usually played down the size of crowds at Gandhi's functions, reported that one hundred thousand people created a white flowing river because all the people joining the procession wore white khadi.

"You are recovering from a fever, Baoji. Adrith Bhaiya is marching; you will get a firsthand account from him."

"I cannot only preach; I must act too. I had fever earlier when Gandhiji called for volunteers for the Dandi satyagraha." Kishan Chand handed Leela an envelope. "Now I am fine. Read this. It came yesterday."

Leela scanned the yellow sheet:

> On May 4, Gandhi ji will inform Lord Irwin, viceroy of India, explaining his intention to march on the Dharasana Salt Works. They expect he and other Congress leaders like Nehru and Sardar Vallabhbhai Patel will be arrested, but even if that happens, the plan is for someone else to lead the march as intended to keep up the pressure on the government.

"Baoji, why you?"

"I am old but not that old. If the police resort to violence, and they will, they will need me because I am old enough to keep hotheaded youngsters from retaliating. Gandhi ji says if we lift even one lathi in violence, we lose."

"You might get hurt, Baoji."

"Don't worry. Volunteers are assigned to move the injured aside to save them from further harm, and protestors following behind will march to the front."

"But you …" Leela visualized the beatings, horrified.

"Abbas Tyabji, seventy-six years old and a retired judge, is leading the march with Gandhi ji's wife, Kasturba. If he gets arrested, Sarojini Naidu is to lead the march. What justification is there for me to stay back?"

Leela reread the letter.

> You must not use violence under any circumstances. You will be beaten, but you must not resist; you must not even raise an arm to ward off blows.

It was signed by the poet-activist Sarojini Naidu.

Tears flowed down Leela's cheeks. "I met Tyabji in Amritsar. At that time, he was at the peak of his career, and he counselled the governor against defending Dyer's brutality. But he was ignored, like you were about partitioning Bengal, and like you, that is when he turned against them. His legal clout enabled your release." Leela returned the telegram. "If Anita were old enough, she would join the march, and I would not stop her. So, I won't stop you either."

"If I land in jail, come and get me. You are good at that," Baoji teased. "Ishaan can manage here."

The protest went ahead as planned. Tyabji and Gandhi's wife, Kasturba, led the march; both were arrested before reaching Dharasana and sentenced to three months in prison. Abbas Tyabji never recovered from the hardships of prison and later, in 1936, when he died at his home in Mussoorie, Gandhi wrote, "Abbas Mian is not dead, though his body rests in the grave. His life is an inspiration for us all."

After their arrests, the peaceful agitation continued with Sarojini Naidu and Maulana Abdul Kalam Azad in the lead. They also faced arrest. More than 1,300 unarmed Indians were severely beaten or killed. For the first time, the world heard because the British were unable to stop Web Miller, an American, from dispatching to the New York World-Telegram:

> On May 22, the world heard his scream of horror: Amazing scenes were witnessed yesterday when over 2,500 Gandhi "volunteers" advanced against the salt pans here in defiance of police regulations. The official government version of the raid, issued today, stated that "from Congress sources it is estimated 170 sustained injuries, but three or four were seriously hurt." About noon yesterday I visited the temporary hospital in the Congress camp and counted over 200 injured lying in rows on the ground. I verified by personal observation that they were suffering injuries. Today even the British owned newspapers give the total number at 320 … The scene at Dharasana during the raid was astonishing and baffling to the Western mind, accustomed to see violence met by violence, to expect a blow to be returned and a fight result. During the morning I saw and heard hundreds of blows inflicted by the police but saw not a single blow returned by the volunteers. So far as I could observe, the volunteers implicitly obeyed Gandhi's creed of non-violence. In no case did I see a volunteer even

> raise an arm to deflect the blows from lathis. There were no outcries from the beaten Swarajists, only groans after they had submitted to their beating …

Miller's report was censored in India. Adrith dressed in white khadi mingled with protesters in the back of the march and spent the day discreetly dispatching eyewitness accounts to local-language papers. By the time it was his turn to face the lathis, it was twilight, and the area was overflowing with the wounded. As he fell, he saw Pitaji bleeding into the soil.

"Thank God you are here, Adi."

Adrith was on his knees, extricating Pitaji from the nullah, when he heard the voice. He looked through the haze and saw a woman wringing her hands, holding back tears. *Only one person calls me Adi.*

"Why are you here, Kamla?"

"Where were you? I searched everywhere."

"I was hiding in the crowd to send dispatches."

"I was bandaging wounds and helping the injured leave this area when I saw your father. After the first blow, they were instructed to move aside, but he kept walking forward. I dragged him away but not before a lathi landed on his head. I bandaged it, but that is all I could do."

"I should have been with him, not in the back."

"Adi, it is not too late. Take him home on the night train. The hospitals here are overflowing, and doctors are overwhelmed." She helped lift the body onto Adrith's shoulder. "I will come to your house in a few days. Maybe your father's injuries are superficial, and with proper care, he will recover."

Adrith had known Kamla Gupta since childhood. Her father had once owned large tracts of land in Dehradun and built a house on East Canal Road near theirs. In college, she had shared his passion for writing, and they traveled together. There was a time when Kamla had wanted to marry Adrith, but he had not been ready, and after that, they met less often. She still participated in protest rallies but had started questioning peaceful resistance as the path to freedom. "Freedom is not given; it is taken," she said, quoting Subhas Chandra Bose. Then she heard that her twenty-one-year-old cousin Bina Das had fired five bullets at Stanley Jackson, the cruel governor presiding at her graduation ceremony in Calcutta. Bina had never held a gun before, and her action was a statement rather than attempted assassination, but she was promptly arrested and sentenced to nine years of rigorous imprisonment. Everyone thought that, like Bhagat Singh, Bina would never come out alive. After that, Kamla became active with a revolutionary youth group in Calcutta. As their ideologies diverged, their relationship became strained: hours of rancorous debate punctuated by moments of passionate bliss.

"Adi, are you OK?"

"I am a fool, Kamla."

"Adi, go home. We can talk later."

"Are you coming to Dehradun?"

Kamla split her time maintaining a hostel for women in Calcutta and looking after her ailing father in Dehradun. It was rumored that the Calcutta home was used to store and courier bombs to revolutionaries, but despite several raids, no evidence was ever uncovered.

"Yes. I will see you in a few days, Adi." Kamla stood on her toes and kissed him. "Now go."

"You saved his life, Adrith. The swelling in his head will reduce," the doctor said.

"No. Kamla saved him. I am the one responsible for his injuries."

"Don't blame yourself," said Samar. "It was Pitaji's choice. The British will continue ruling, and we can't do anything about it."

"Yes, we can, Samar. I am not like you." Adrith imagined blows raining on his father's head, stooping shoulders, and frail form. *What if Kamla had been in the back with him?* "I have to carry on Pitaji's legacy."

Kishan Chand's physical injuries healed, but the prolonged confinement weakened his spirit. By the time he could sit, the only memories he retained were those of his youth.

"Leela, where is Radha? Tell her I want to tell her a joke. Then she will come."

"Baoji, she sent this daal-roti for you—the way you like it." Leela set the platter near the bed, and Samar fed him spoonful by spoonful.

Kishan Chand stayed unresponsive. Adrith could not bear to watch his giant of a father reduced to rubble. At mealtimes, he disappeared, and when asked, said he was visiting friends or in the library writing letters and reading manuscripts.

"Kamla says nonviolence is futile against the British because they promise freedom while enforcing oppression. Remember how Pitaji's role model died? The superintendent ordered the lathi charge and personally assaulted Lajpat Rai."

Samar, as the eldest, spoke for the family. "Violence begets violence, Adrith. Last week, Bhagat Singh, who plotted vengeance for Rai's killing, was executed by hanging. How well did that work?"

"Execution at twenty-three makes him a hero in my book."

"Yes, he is *shaheed*, but what changed? We must live to fight. You can't fight if you are dead."

"Bhagat Singh's action has inspired the new generation. He was a scholar and used his time in jail to write. You should read it. He died happy and regretted not a single day of his life."

"Pitaji has no regrets either."

"Yes, but I do. Subhas Chandra Bose, a protégé of Gandhi, now leads a Congress Volunteer Corps that enlists people with military skills. Kamla told me she has joined Chhatri Sangha, a revolutionary group in Calcutta."

"But you wield a pen," Samar argued. "What would you do?"

"I have been reading *Swaraj* and *The Indian Struggle* by Bose. He managed to get it printed in England, but in India it is banned, and he is living in exile. I will print his book."

"Not here. We get raided regularly."

"Well then in Calcutta."

"Pitaji would tell you to do anything, except use violence."

"Samar, you are not Pitaji; don't tell me what to do."

"You are right." Samar held Adrith till his anger turned into tears.

"I can't stay here and watch Pitaji. Do you understand?"

"Yes," Samar said without conviction. "It is not long now. We will win."

"Amma, is Adrith Tauji going to jail? Like Dadu?"

"No, Anita. He is going to Calcutta."

"You are hiding things from me again, Amma."

"I told Tauji I would help him like I helped your dadu."

"Dadu needs you here," Anita said. "I can help Tauji."

"Yes, but this time it must be kept secret, Anita. Do you understand?"

Like his father years before, Adrith left Dehradun without giving an address or return date.

On his deathbed, Kishan Chand put Anita in charge of *Doon Patrika*. "Your gift from a jailbird." He grinned, flashing the old fighting spirit.

# 19

## *Dehradun New Cantonment, 1935*

"Is it profit or patriotism that drives your request, Mrs. Chand?" Lady Joanna Harrington embodied classic imperial condescension as she plumped cushions of floral velour adorning wickerwork armchairs. She sank in, as if relieving a back weary of its burden, and exhaled a rhetorical full stop.

Leela gazed steadily. "By the same token, Lady Joanna, is the British urge to colonize driven by plunder or patriotism?"

Ishaan had advised against this tea party, but she had insisted. Not wanting to reveal the real reason, she cited a plausible one, saying, "I know they represent the Raj, but for our school, I can handle some sneers. I won't lose my composure." But she had.

Lady Harrington sat up. In her own native way, the woman was regal despite being dressed like a commoner. Her head was uncovered—unlike the jewel-encrusted ranis and decorous daughters she was used to meeting. Usually a charging rhinoceros, she paused midstride.

"Harrumph," she said, no longer radiating patronizing tedium.

Leela switched on the charm. "Lady Joanna, I believe you know who would be most qualified to teach English at our school. Whether I am motivated by profit or patriotism, it is certainly not plunder I have in mind. We recompense our staff handsomely." She paused and said, "Chand Industries fills imperial tax coffers because we can monetize the local economy. We take the risk; you reap the rewards. We give loans during the planting season and purchase the harvest. In a drought year, we suffer but not you. Dehradun is a district magistrate's dream, don't you agree?"

"Why come to me?" spat Lady Harrington.

"An institution that combines the best of British and Indian education in your district would be a feather in your cap, I think."

Lord Harrington arrived and ended the uncomfortable silence with a booming "Good afternoon. Good afternoon." He entered the side gate, crossed the expansive, softer than silk on bare feet *doob* runner grass lawn bordered by immaculate, fragrant flowerbeds, pecked his wife on both cheeks, and turned to the native woman.

Leela saw Ishaan enter, and behind him tripped dainty Elizabeth Harrington—the object of her interest. She rose from her chair, stepped forward, and tilted her head in a generalized greeting.

"Ishaan has not done justice. You are lovelier by far, Mrs. Chand." Lord Harrington eyed Leela's lustrous black curls and aquiline nose and moved his gaze down her long neck to where it dipped into her sari blouse of green and gold. "Brilliant."

Lady Harrington was having none of it. "Have you met Elizabeth, Leela? She is on holiday before joining college back home."

Leela allowed the magistrate to brush the top of her hand with his lips and sizeable gray mustache before rescuing it. She folded her palms into a namaste. She acknowledged Ishaan and Elizabeth with a nod, then smiled at Lord Harrington. He was not much taller than her.

"Your home is a paradise, Lord Harrington. Tell me, is there a mango grove nearby? During flowering season, we call it *baur*—the time when trees are laden with tiny blooms before turning into fruit. The *koyals* and bulbuls sing their sweetest melodies. I have not heard so many birds in a long time."

"You too, Leela?" broke in Lady Harrington and bustled the company back to cushioned comfort. "Ishaan took Elizabeth on a birdwatching trip, and she returned flushed with their exertions. Quite beastly, I must say. Why would anyone risk tramping in this heat and dust?"

"Lady Joanna, our valley is a birder's paradise. A diversity of habitats makes it possible to identify over four hundred unique species." Leela turned to Elizabeth. "Perhaps you know B. B. Omaston of the Imperial Forest Service? He has become quite an authority on the subject and has written of his adventures in our valley."

"No. I have just arrived from England," Elizabeth replied, her eyes fixed on Ishaan as he chatted with her father.

"You must read his article "Birds Nesting in the Tons Valley." I believe he is working on a book: *Birds of Dehra Dun and the Adjacent Hills*."

Elizabeth continued following Ishaan with flirtatious eyes, a teenager determined on romance.

"I know BBO," sniffed Mama Harrington, "but hobnobbing with the natives! No boundaries in his fervor—running around like he does." Lady Harrington seemed disappointed in this servant of the Raj who enjoyed his tenure far too much.

"As children, we scoured the valley birdwatching. We drew new species in a book, identified them when we got home, and whoever spotted the most won. Elizabeth, you must not encourage Ishaan, or he will drag you uphill and downdale with no concession for your delicate complexion. Your mother is right; our Indian sun can be painful for the white-skinned."

"Mama, where is our tea?" Elizabeth pouted, ignored Leela, lifted the bell sitting on the low stand, and shook it vigorously. "All this talk of tramping has made me thirsty." Then turning to Ishaan, eyebrows arched in a gesture that could be called seductive in a sophisticated woman but was at odds with her teenage plumpness, she giggled and said, "Is it only birds that interest you, Ishaan?"

Lady Harrington pursed her lips in a thin line of annoyance.

A clattering of crockery preceded the frail woman wrapped in a sari made threadbare by multiple washings. She carried a tray loaded with a steaming teapot, cups, plates, scones, and lemonade. She tottered to a stop, regained her balance, and lowered the burden on the center table without undue noise or spillage.

"Where is Usmaan?" Lady Harrington barked. "How many times have I told you to stay in the kitchen? You know very well only serving staff is allowed here." She shuddered as imagined boiling water poured into her lap. "You almost dropped the tray."

The woman muttered indistinctly about Usmaan being bedridden and hastily withdrew.

"Ishaan, how do you deal with your servants—so lazy and unreliable, feigning illness or emergency every day. I am told the Portuguese brought their own servants to Goa. Is that true?"

"Yes, Portuguese nobles brought slaves with them along with other possessions. Europe has a tradition of slavery, but in India, we do not, so once in Goa, the slaves, African usually, ran away or demanded freedom." Ishaan took a glass of lemonade and wandered off, as if to inspect the flowerbeds, and then vanished behind the hedge.

The party settled, the unpleasantness apparently forgotten. Leela elaborated on her school plans; Lady Harrington promised she would contact her friends at Eton. Leela expressed gratitude by saying how enriching it was to know multiple languages, that the library in Radha Vilas was well stocked with the latest English and American publications in addition to Indian books.

"Elizabeth, you may enjoy a visit to our library," Leela said and discovered that Elizabeth had disappeared too.

Lady Harrington dismissed the library invitation.

"I understand Indians needing to learn our language, Leela, but why would the English learn any another?" She extracted a paper from a pile and flung it across. "Lies. All lies."

Leela was glad she did not recognize *Doon Patrika*. Then she saw Ishaan enter the garden.

"Thank you for a lovely afternoon. We must beg our leave, Lady Joanna." Leela waved to Ishaan. "But do ask Elizabeth on my behalf. She might find something of interest in Radha Vilas."

# 20

*Majhra Farms, 1935*

"How could you, Ishaan?" Leela said, getting into the car, barely able to speak. "In everyone's presence?"

Ishaan drove off the property, waving goodbyes, and waited till the gates closed behind them before asking, "How could I what?"

"Elizabeth. The entire town is talking about you two. And in their own house—how could you?" Leela choked.

Ishaan laughed. "My. My. The unflappable Leela is perturbed. Tell me what bothers you—that there might be truth to the rumors or that it might hurt your chances of landing a schoolmaster?"

Realizing her mistake, Leela switched tactics. "What do you think, Ishaan? You understand me. Why don't you hazard a guess?"

"I think you wanted to see Elizabeth, so you cooked up this ridiculous schoolmaster story. We can hire better staff without their help, and you know it. Yet you insisted on this charade with Lady Harrington."

Leela sat mute.

"So, I am right." Ishaan chuckled. "Elizabeth the English rose. Is that your verdict, Leela?"

"You are right about the visit but not the rest." Leela hoped she had not been as transparent to Lady Joanna as she was to Ishaan. "I was upset." She looked out the window to hide her distress.

"If you must know, I disappeared to go see Usmaan and his family. He is ill indeed. I gave his wife some money and will send our doctor as soon as we get home." Ishaan looked at Leela, then grinned. "As for Elizabeth, she followed me. What could I do? That is why I returned from that back gate. Anyway, I was gone a few minutes—not enough time to merit your suspicions."

"I thought Elizabeth was older. What I saw was a bored teenager confused by the trappings of her parents' complicity in upholding exploitation. It is her way of rebelling."

"What? You don't think she hungers for me?"

"I didn't say that. What interests me is how you feel about her."

"Find out for yourself. Join us on our next birdwatching trip." Leela hesitated, so he issued a challenge. "I dare you."

"I look forward to it, Ishaan."

"Right then. Irrespective of your findings, it would serve to squash rumors floating around town, wouldn't it? Do you agree, Leela?

Was this Ishaan's unconventional way of inviting her out, or did he mean to humiliate her with a ridiculous display of juvenile flirtation?

"Whatever. And I will invite the English rose to visit our library—erudition may add fragrance to form—and you are welcome to join us, Ishaan. I dare you."

The outing day turned out to be unseasonably hot, and Elizabeth arrived well past the morning hour, red and tired. "There was some kind of pileup on the way—a demonstration—so we took a detour," she said, dropping into an armchair. "Mama forbade the trip, so here I am, Ishaan."

"She was right. A muggy day is too much for trekking through sal forests."

"Ishaan, you promised me an outing." Elizabeth pouted.

"Have some water." Leela pointed to a tray. "We could still go somewhere."

"Anywhere. Do not make me go back home. Mama is driving me insane. She does not behave like this in England."

Ishaan and Leela discussed alternatives.

"How about a trip to our farm?" Leela suggested. "The irrigation channels on the farm attract a variety of waterfowl. And we can stay cool in shady groves. We can picnic too."

Anita heard *farm* and clamored to join. Other children came and voted for it.

"How about it, Elizabeth?" Ishaan asked.

"Not what I had in mind," Elizabeth said without enthusiasm.

Umang, who had returned recently from England, came to see what the commotion was about. He opted in. "It will be like the old days," he said.

Elizabeth perked up. "Umang, I did not know Ishaan had a younger brother."

Ishaan drove his car, and the rest piled into tongas or walked. The original trip for two morphed into a family outing typical of Leela's early years in Dehradun. *And I have an Englishwoman to thank for it.*

No longer expected to play a daughter of the Raj, Elizabeth dipped in canals to cool off along with the motley group, ate with her hands, ran barefoot in the fields, dozed under the shade of a mango tree, and when Anita sat on the old farm horse, she taught her how to ride. When Ishaan and Umang carried the children piggyback and raced, Elizabeth joined the games. Too soon, it was dusk and time to head home.

"Elizabeth, you remind me of friends in college," Umang said. "Go back to England."

"What do you mean, Umang?"

"Did you enjoy yourself today?"

"Yes, much more than the birdwatching trips with Ishaan, which annoy Mama so much. Now that I think about it, I felt like I belonged. You all were so kind to me, yet Mama says nasty things about everyone, and that makes me feel bad."

"If we met in a Whites Only club, would you have the courage to stand up to your mama?"

"Of course, I would. I feel closer to your family than my own."

"Exactly, but in a few months, you will change; instead of family, you will see me as foreign, and in your heart, you will know you are wrong. That is why I say go back; romanticize the Raj if you will, buy don't become an enforcer of the Raj."

By the time they returned to East Canal Road, Elizabeth understood what ailed her at home—not India; it was what Mama had become in serving queen and country.

That summer, Umang taught Elizabeth tennis. Anita taught her Hindi. Elizabeth taught Anita English, and one day Anita told her about Sister Mary and Dadu being jailed for asking a question. "Never stop asking questions," said Elizabeth, and later, after Lord Harrington was assigned a new district, Elizabeth continued visiting the house on East Canal Road—a white woman who was happier being brown.

Leela and Ishaan bought an extensive property on Rajpur Road. Leela consulted the priest and chose an auspicious day to shift the school—twenty-five full-time students now—and the four resident teachers, including Ayla, Masterji, and an Englishwoman to its new premises. Prospective students and their parents clapped when Samar, the family elder, handed Leela the scissors and she snipped the ribbon on the door of the entrance hall. They toured the grounds and stayed for the festivities: a buffet followed by a variety of entertainment.

"It was a grand party, Leela," Ishaan said on the drive home. "You must be exhausted."

"Ishaan, you made it possible. I feel like a weight has been lifted off my shoulders. I am tired but happy."

Once home, everyone congratulated one another and disappeared for the night. Leela paced in her room, not ready for bed. She walked into Ishaan's chambers.

"Can you help me with this?" She pointed to her back. "My blouse seems tangled in the necklace."

Ishaan was undressing for the night. In all the years since that day when he came home with Ayla in tow—Leela had not once come to his bedroom. She still wore the green and red sari from the party, but the blouse exposed one bare shoulder. She had taken the pins out of the chignon, so ebony curls tumbled down her back.

"What is it, Leela?"

"See this hook? Is it stuck on something?" Leela moved close till her shoulder blades grazed his chest.

Ishaan hesitated. "Let's see." He lifted the hair off her neck—the sexy, musky attar of tuberoses filled his nostrils.

"It's tangled in your hair—must have happened when you uncoiled your bun." He unhooked the blouse with ease, reexperiencing past moments of ecstasy. "All done."

But Leela stayed in his arms.

"Let me help you with your shirt." She unbuttoned his kurta; with her fingertips, she traced *I want you* on his bare skin. Slowly.

Deliberately. Then again and again till he shuddered and slumped into the hollow of her neck.

"Where is Anita?"

"Anita has her own room." Leela circled his waist, squeezed tight, and buried her face in his chest. "And l have lost precious time that I need to make up for."

# PART IV
## *Anita*

Quit India stamp. Canceled stamp from India commemorating the Quit India Movement of 1942, in which civil disobedience was used to try to gain independence from the British.

# 21

## *Calcutta 1931–1942*

"Look, Amma!" Anita waved an envelope as she ran in. "It is from Adrith Tauji."

"Hug first?" Leela stalled, basking in her daughter's exuberance. "Let me see."

When Adrith walked out of the house on East Canal Road, Samar thought he would be back in a few weeks. Pitaji's flight to Allahabad and subsequent return had achieved legendary status in his mind. Adrith was like Pitaji; he would return once he was done grieving.

Two weeks passed, and Adrith did not come back. Neither did he write. A few months later when Kishan Chand died, the family performed the cremation and ceremonial rites befitting a beloved patriarch, but Adrith was not there to lend a shoulder. Samar, Ishaan, and Umang carried his *arthi* to the cremation grounds.

Leela rationalized his absence. *Adrith Bhaiya paid his respects before he went to Calcutta. He held himself responsible for Baoji's injuries and started studying Subhas Chandra Bose. Hadn't Bose become disillusioned with peaceful protests in the 1920s and 1930s?*

Samar had his own logic. *For all the fire and brimstone Adrith puts in his pen, he never lifted a swatter to a fly. Bose is an intellectual, erudite and engaging, and I am sure that is his charm. I hope his influence will wear off with time and he will return home.*

Ishaan supported his absence too. *Pitaji and Adrith are still on the same side, but Adrith is fighting in different ways now. He will come home when he is ready. The best thing he can do is fill the void Pitaji's passing has created with new purpose. And that cannot happen at a peace rally.*

Leela folded the letter and put it back in the envelope.

"What does it say, Amma?" Anita tugged at her mother's pallu. "Or give it back, and I will read it myself."

"Tauji has joined Bose's army and will be leaving for Burma." The words were out of Leela's mouth before she realized the enormity of the news. "Postmarked Calcutta but no return address."

"Amma, we have to stop Tauji. He is a writer, not a military man."

"Yes, Anita. I will talk to Papa."

Ishaan wrote to friends in Calcutta and acquired an address. They said Adrith endangered his life daily by giving fiery speeches in underground gatherings about his belief that Britain's stand against Nazism and fascism was hypocrisy, as they were themselves responsible for blatant human rights violations in the colonies; that they would rule India unless faced by a military stronger than theirs.

What to do? The family caucused: Adrith would not listen to Samar or Ishaan. Umang, as the younger brother, might at least gain an audience.

"I will go," Umang said. "I know some journalists who are sympathetic to the Indian National Army ideology. When he sees me in person, maybe he will understand our concerns."

"Umang Chacha, please take me with you," said Anita, thirteen going on nineteen. "Tauji won't say no to me."

"You are a journalist," Umang reasoned with his brother. "Bose's army, Azad Hind Fauj, has now merged with the Indian National Army, so he has no shortage of firebrands; what he needs is combat expertise. Soldiers suffering discrimination and food shortages in the British Indian Army, eager to fight for India, are lining up to join. What can you do?"

"I do not have a military background, so I am getting trained. They will place me somewhere."

"Your pen is the most powerful weapon you have. Why not influence with your pen? No one in the family will ask you to change your views. We are all fighting in our different ways to free India."

"I still write, and some even get past the censors. The *Statesman* is published here. I can send dispatches to Bombay and Madras for the *Times* of India, and the *Hindu* from here. I also write in Bengali and Hindi for local papers."

"Tauji, why can't you do your work in Dehradun?"

"Dehradun is a military town. Even your Umang Chacha is a doctor in the military. And Baoji's paper is about peaceful protests. I cannot change its ideology."

"I can. Dadu gave the paper to me. I can do what I want—"

"We worry about you, about your safety," Umang interrupted. "We came to help."

"The Indian National Army needs doctors too. Why don't you join me in Burma, Umang?"

Finally, it was Anita who broke the stalemate. "We came to take you back. If you won't return, at least stay in Calcutta, Tauji."

"I can't promise that. Besides, you are safer in Dehradun without me. I do miss having a printing press though. My notes are messy." He hesitated. "When Bose was exiled in Vienna, he relied on memory to write. *The Indian Struggle* was published in Europe back in 1934, but in India, the government has been quick to ban it."

"Can they do that?"

"They did. When Bose returned to India, they seized the manuscript, saying it 'encourages terrorism and violence.' I have read parts and found it very thoughtful. Even English journalists have reviewed it positively, but if I said the same thing, the *Statesman* would not publish it."

"I have an idea," Anita said. "Dadu's press is at the farm. I will fix it, but only if you promise not to decamp to some swamp in Burma—and write every week."

"No way," said Umang, shocked at this turn of events. "Anita is a child. Leela will be furious. You cannot ask this of us, Bhaiya."

"It's not your decision, Umang. Boys younger than Anita choose to enlist in our army. It is a need of the hour."

"Chacha, please," Anita pleaded with Umang. "Don't you remember Sister Mary's story? Amma says sometimes it is okay to act without permission."

"It is your time to promise, Anita," Adrith said. "Can you be careful?"

"Yes." Anita nodded. "It will be our secret."

Adrith stayed on in Calcutta and promised to write regularly. Anita and Umang returned home, knowing it was the best possible outcome.

"Anita, your Tauji will be happier in Calcutta," Ishaan said. "At least he is not in Burma."

To Umang, he gave a brotherly pat. "Good work. Adrith would surely be lying dead in the Burma swamps if you two had not gone. He only knows how to wield a pen—cannot fight to save life or limb. I won every bout we ever had."

# 22

*Burma 1936–1942*

Viceroy Linlithgow declared India's entry into the Second War in September 1939, making vague promises to leave India after war ended. Britain needed India's men to fight, and India's strategic location in Asia would prevent the onslaught of Japanese soldiers into Europe if Britain lost the fight in Burma. More than two and a half million Indians fought against Germany and Japan in Europe and Asia. One of them was Ravindra Rathore. He was deployed to Italy as senior officer in the ten-thousand-strong Mahratta Light Infantry Indian Division. He poured the pride he felt in his men in letters to Ishaan:

> You would empathize with my sappers and miners. They are the civil engineers essential to every military formation and responsible for building

> roads, bridges, accommodations, and for laying and clearing minefields. No battle group can function effectively in action without them. I crisscross the treacherous Italian Alps guiding infantry, artillery, and cavalry (tanks) supporting the infantry up front. Like you at home, I make sure the beans, bullets, and bandages—food, ammunition, medical supplies—get to our men. I am a traffic cop too, directing various units to their different locations in Europe.

Ravi's tone was always upbeat though in one of his last letters, he wrote:

> In combat it is so chaotic that the Tommy invented a mnemonic describing the chaos as SNAFU, which means Situation Normal, All F****d Up!

Ishaan's friend was killed fighting a foreign war on foreign soil. India's demand for an orderly British withdrawal, later dubbed Quit India Movement, was met with imprisonment of all national and local leaders without trial. A complete news ban was imposed. Congress members spent the rest of the war in prison, out of contact and unable to rally the disheartened. The British Broadcasting Service blared daily on British heroism, while more than thirty-six thousand Indian soldiers lost their lives, an equal number were wounded, and sixty-seven thousand were taken prisoners of war. Indian doctors and nurses tended the injured on British soil and in other foreign countries. Throughout the war effort, Indians were paid less, endured harsher conditions, often faced discrimination at the hands of their fellow British officers, and were viewed as outcasts among the larger social club.

Indian journalists had no choice but to bend the truth in

dispatches sent outside India—a survival tactic that led eventually to a false narrative becoming truth. Adrith would not be party to misinformation, so he wrote Anita to say he had kept his part of the pact, but now it was time for the trenches.

He left Calcutta to join Bose in Burma.

Umang resigned from his position in Dehradun to join the Indian Military Hospital in Burma. Anita could not be stopped from accompanying Umang Chacha; she could work as a nurse, she said.

"You have no training, Anita. How can you help?" Leela objected.

"Umang Chacha is teaching me. I can already give an injection and bandage wounds. Just yesterday, I made a tourniquet. I may not be the best, but I know I can help. Don't stop me, Amma."

The three Chands—journalist, doctor, and nurse—met in Rangoon.

The frontier region between Burma and India was impassable country, with very few navigable routes through the jungle-clad hills. Living conditions were miserable for civilians, and the troops faced food shortages and scarce medical supplies. Umang and Anita tended the injured twenty-four hours every day and asked no questions. Adrith stayed in hill camps, followed the troops into battle, and sent firsthand accounts to the Calcutta underground press. The three met in the city market every few days.

It was a heady year; they were winning: Umang saved lives, Anita brought smiles to the sickest of soldiers, and Adrith sent dispatches no one else could. In 1942, the Indian National Army, led by the charismatic and capable Netaji Bose, made significant inroads into India through Burma, with the goal of liberating India. However, their progress frightened the British, so, like they did in 1857, they cut off food supplies to Bengal and confiscated existing stock. The idea was to starve the entire region, so that the incoming army would have to compete for food with the local population. A horrific time, the 1942–1943 Bengal famine, gripped the country.

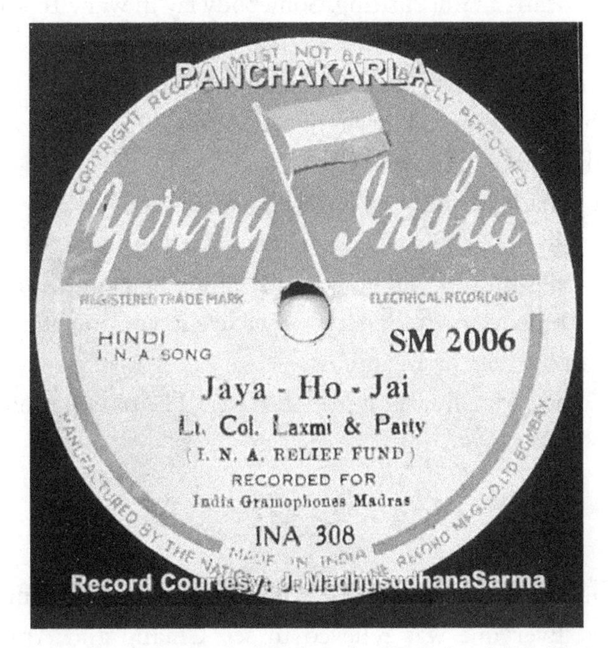


Record cover—national anthem by Lt. Colonel Lakshmi Sehgal, sung in 1943 after winning in Port Blair, capital of the Andaman and Nicobar Islands, a union territory of India.

One day, Adrith did not come to the market. Umang heard a man had been seen in the jungle by the river—apparently drunk. In the dark of night, Umang and Anita went to the area and found Adrith in a ditch—reeking of alcohol. That must have been what caused the accident, people had said, except Anita knew Tauji never drank.

"Whoever killed him poured *taadi* to make it look like an accident," she said.

"Yes. There were signs of a skirmish as if multiple people jumped on him." Umang brought his fingers to his lips. "Shh …" Umang examined the body and found his neck broken—but not the way it would from a fall; it had been snapped. "Listen."

They heard a faint rustling. Somebody lay in wait. To kill other soldiers.

"Hurry. We must leave." Umang saw no reason to stay any longer; his sole responsibility now was Anita. "They are waiting in case soldiers have followed us here."

"We can't leave Tauji. Who will cremate him?"

"We will have a pooja when we get back. I promise. Eventually, our medical uniforms will not save us, Anita. Someone has seen us; they will come to town. Better that we live to continue his fight in India than die here in an ambush."

They dug a shallow grave by the river. The only personal item Anita took: his pen.

Ishaan had heard about Adrith's fate from his contacts in Calcutta. Everyone was relieved to see Umang and Anita, and Adrith's cremation pooja was a private affair.

Anita continued as a nurse. "I couldn't save my Tauji," she said. "Maybe I can save someone else's."

Dehradun hospitals swelled with an influx of the war wounded. With the help of Indian officers, Umang launched a campaign that Indian National Army prisoners of war be accorded the same treatment as British Indian soldiers. "Indians are fighting for India, no matter what the army is named," he said.

"Indian leaders have been negotiating for decades. England was to hand over the reins to India after the war, but they have again reneged," said Ishaan.

Anita was furious. "Tauji was right, Papa."

Reports from Calcutta said the Indian National Army forces had been winning, so the British caused a second Bengal famine to stop them. Food shortages in Calcutta led mobs to storm ration centers. The *Statesman* talked of losses in the Indian ranks. British newspapers crowed about the valor of their army. Eventually, more than four million Indians starved to death, and the Indian National Army stopped its march to Calcutta.

"Good, Pitaji is not here to see such treachery," Ishaan agreed. "Even his beliefs would be shaken. Months have gone by, and there is no substantive talk of independence. The English are exulting in postwar euphoria. Adding insult to injury, they have begun trials of the Indian National Army soldiers. I am happy railway and postal workers are going on strikes all over India. They will have to stop."

Having heard promises from their pacifist leadership for more than twenty years, there was growing impatience among the civilians and the military. The Indian Air Force, the British Indian Army, and the Royal Indian Navy joined forces and led an attack, and for a few triumphant days in February 1946, the English flag was replaced by flags of the Congress Party and Muslim League. Fear of their combined strength, many believe, is what really caused the British to free India.

# 23

*Dehradun, 1942–1946*

Sergeant Ludlow shifted his weight from one foot to the other. Not uncomfortable but curious. The old manservant's ramrod posture and curt nod stated in no uncertain terms that the sergeant would not be admitted into the house; he was to stay on the open veranda. As for his subordinate, a native constable, he was to wait outside the iron gates and shush the horses. The old man had set the tone: polite but in no way obsequious. Sergeant Ludlow wished he had not made such a production of his arrival. After all, there were no native hordes, the ones who appeared in his training manuals, to fend in this quiet mansion. Ah well! He had been in the country for only one month. Better to be safe than sorry.

He paced the black-and-white, square-patterned marble veranda. He marveled at the height of the twelve columns supporting massive wooden beams. This was just about the most magnificently appointed entrance he had ever seen. He was admiring a dozen antlers mounted high on the wall when footsteps approached.

"Sorry to make you wait." The confident, youthful voice carried across the length of the veranda.

Sergeant Ludlow turned around: the girl stood much too close for his comfort. He took a step back.

"Dadu is overprotective. He is not my real grandfather, but I call him Dadu. He said I should not meet you, but here I am." She lifted an arm and pointed in the general direction of the ceiling. "Those *barasingha* antlers—aren't they impressive? My grandfather paid atrocious amounts for them to the strapped-for-cash Indian royals. He did not hunt, at least not deer." The young woman smiled genially. "I am so glad to meet you."

"Harrumph ..." Sergeant Ludlow stammered. "Eh ... er ..."

"My father has already left for work, and I heard horses neighing. I had to see for myself. Few people come to our house riding these days. I knew it was not a tonga because there were no bells jangling. Have you come to see Papa?"

"Sergeant Ludlow, ma'am. Imperial Police. I am here to see Mr. Chand."

"Yes, that's Papa. He is not here. I am his daughter, Anahita. How can I help?"

The young woman did not hold out her hand or fold her palms in a formal namaste. Instead, she smiled as if he was paying a social visit. *Not making it easy.* Nobody had instructed Sergeant Ludlow on police protocol in apprehending friendly natives. "I would like to talk to an adult member of Mr. Chand's family."

"Then aren't you lucky I convinced Dadu to let me see you. I am here, an adult member of the Chand family."

"You are served," Sergeant Ludlow said abruptly. He extracted a document from his satchel and formally gave it to the girl who said she was an adult. "A warrant to search the premises. You have a printing press?"

"Yes, of course, we have a printing press. We are publishers after all." Anita read the paper carefully. "And it doesn't require a genius to figure out our company's name." Ebony eyes twinkled in mischief.

"Chand Publishers?" Sergeant Ludlow stammered. He had been told native women were quite unattractive.

"Bingo!" Housie was a gambling game made popular at church socials and was now played at cantonment clubs too, but the Englishman did not understand the reference, so Anita elaborated. "The board above the shop announces it in three languages: Hindi, Urdu, and English. You can't miss it."

"No. My orders state this address."

"You mean the factory, don't you? It is on Rajpur Road. I can take you there if you wish. You don't need a new warrant."

"No. My orders are to search the residence and confiscate the press." To regain a semblance of imperial authority, he said, "HQ levies fines and sentences first and then conducts a trial. I am not here to make an arrest."

Anita wrinkled her brows. "Confiscate the press?" Then her eyes shone. "I see now. Follow me, Sergeant. No need to call your man—unless you imagine I would assault you." Without waiting for consent, she turned and led the way inside. "I will show you where we hide it. Good, you brought your horse; it is heavy."

Sergeant Ludlow, refusing to be drawn into banter, drew himself into proper police posture. "Yes, ma'am. It is always prudent to assist the law."

"You may call me Anita. Only Amma calls me by my full name."

They walked through an expansive, handsomely carpeted hall furnished with elaborate teak furniture. The ceiling was three stories high. Large oil portraits and sepia family photographs hung high above. Walking behind Anita, Sergeant Ludlow noticed her hair was still wet from the bath, and drops of water trickled on her back, making the white cotton blouse transparent.

His eyes transfixed on the barely visible outlines of what looked like a bra. Where had he heard barrack laughs about bare-breasted native women? No, this was the country where they flung women into flaming pyres. Then where were her yards of veil? This one had not even covered her head. And she spoke English!

Ludlow could imagine no one throwing this young woman onto a pyre. *I should lift her though—to see if I would need one arm or both.*

As if reading his mind, the woman in front quickened her pace, unlatched a carved walnut door, and flung it open. "There it is. On the far end."

A library: every wall lined with books and manuscripts of all shapes and sizes. Some titles were in English; others in languages he could not read. A man's portrait on the opposite wall dominated the room. Below it gleamed a glass case enclosing what looked like well-polished machinery.

*The printing press?* Sergeant Ludlow had never seen a printing press before.

"When you confiscate the press, do me a favor, Sergeant. Please confiscate the portrait too. Oil and canvas will burn well. A bonfire might be as much fun as a hanging, don't you think? You can celebrate with a scotch and soda on a job well done for Her Majesty. Or is it gin and tonic for you, Sergeant? Chand Distillers stocks all military canteens. I can have some sent to you. Complimentary, of course."

Ludlow's training told him to take charge.

"Ma'am, our informant has placed the origin of material banned by the government to this house." He glanced around unenthusiastically. "I must search the room."

"Please do. And take your time. I will stay and translate if the need arises. Grandfather's paper is in Hindi and Bengali. Every issue published is archived. On his deathbed, he gave me the paper to manage, but in 1934, the press broke, so we enshrined it. Now I have other interests."

Sergeant Ludlow inspected the room: Dickens and Shakespeare, jousted Tagore, Pritam, Twain. He could not read the foreign titles, but there was still a lifetime of material for him here.

"Half the material is in English, like engineering manuals. Also, grandfather from my mother's side practiced law in Allahabad High Court." The woman practically beamed as she continued. "So his briefs are in English. You can read those. He won every one of his cases, so there is bound to be some material you could write about in your report. We can't disappoint HQ, can we?"

Ludlow inspected the glass case and examined the portrait.

"Tell me, Sergeant, when did you arrive in India? I see you have a lot to learn about dealing with us natives."

"Where do you keep your current records and manuscripts?"

"This way. On my worktable." Anita led him to another part of the library. "In my spare time, I oversee children's books—for our school. You have heard? We have a school too, but it is not called Chand School. You could probably guess, but I will tell you anyway. Amma named it Das Vidya Mandir."

Ludlow thought it best to hold his tongue.

Anita held out a manuscript. "Tales from Panchatantra. Do you know the tale of the tiger and the cows? As long as the cows were together in a herd, the tiger could not harm them, but one day the cows fought. The tiger got his chance and ate the cows one by one. Kipling defends Shere Khan by saying he represented law and order. Like you, Sergeant. Your government knows the story well, though we Indians need frequent reminding."

"It is in English." Ludlow flipped through the pages. "Why?"

"Kipling based *Jungle Book* on our stories, which are written in local languages. Shere Khan is sher, Bagheera is bagh, Baloo bhalu, and so on. He did not bother to hide what he did, knowing his word trumped ours. So, I thought, why not write our ancient folklore in English?" Anita smiled charmingly. "Do you think these books make Kipling look bad? Can I be charged with sedition because I am exposing his sources?"

Ludlow had never been impressed with Kipling's intellect. He thought "The White Man's Burden" was not only poor poetry but also pure imperialist hogwash. He held back a chuckle: *And if she is the burden, I would love to carry her.*

Anita continued, "Though I do like this quote from Kipling:

> I keep six honest serving men,
> They taught me all I know.
> Theirs names are What and Why and When,
> And How, Where and Who.

I wonder, have you ever met Why?"

Sergeant Ludlow parried, "Didn't he also say, '*For the female of the species is deadlier than the male*'? Which story is that one from?"

Anita ignored the question and picked another manuscript. "Or how about this? I am translating a book called Bhagavad Gita, but I have a big problem: I cannot read Sanskrit. So many in my generation do not know our own languages. I started learning but still have a long way to go. On top of that, we do not have one book like your Bible. We have so many books that we do not need a religion to define our culture and way of life."

Sergeant Ludlow covered her hand, holding the book longer than necessary.

"Miss Chand, I will report to my superiors and get back to you on the matter of the printing press."

"Better." Anita laughed. "Not as good as Anita, but much better than ma'am. You must come back. There are godowns behind the main house, and I can open those for you. Grandfather maintained stables and a cowshed there at one time, but now who knows what we might find. We keep them free of dust and mites, so you will be safe, Sergeant."

"Is that right?" He scanned the warrant in pretend concern. "This does not mention stables, cowsheds, or godowns. I will return with proper authorization."

"I look forward to it. We can explore together."

"Yes. This matter is not closed." Sergeant Ludlow clicked heels. Anita looked impressed.

Sergeant Ludlow thought if all his assignments were this much fun, he was never leaving India for his boring life back in England.

At the dinner table, Ishaan raged, "How dare he come to my home. I will see to it he is directly dismissed from his post."

To Munshi Ram, he said, "How could you, Munshiji? Why did you even let him enter the gate?"

"It was all my fault, Papa," Anita interrupted. "I forced Dadu, and besides, Sergeant Ludlow was quite respectful, calling me ma'am this ma'am that. Half the time, I was turning around to see if Amma had come in from behind and he was talking to her."

"You were in danger. Anything could have happened."

"Papa, you are so cautious that I was never in any danger." Anita knew her father sent medical supplies and munitions to Calcutta and Burma, but he kept it strictly off the records and stored nothing at home.

Leela had been quiet so far, but Ishaan needed her support.

"Your papa is cautious, but what about you, Anita? How sensible are you?"

"I had so much fun today. Poor Sergeant Ludlow! He is new to India and yet to learn Raj manners. In fact, I invited him to come again. We have so much to talk about. He is quite handsome and not much older than I am."

"He probably failed high school and joined the police to escape England," Leela said. "Give him time. In six months, he will be all red and bluster. Very unattractive in a man." Then she said, turning to Ishaan, "Or a woman."

Ishaan laughed. "I feel sorry for Ludlow." He knew Anita added a book or two of her own to every shipment bound for Calcutta.

"Don't encourage her, Ishaan. She takes after you with that sassy talk. You handle her."

"I can handle myself, thank you very much," Anita said. "Ask Sergeant Ludlow."

"I know you can, Anita." Ishaan turned to Leela and said, "For sweet-talking people and getting them to do what she wants, she takes after you. The best I could have done was break a few imperial bones, and they would have mended much too soon."

"You always exaggerate, Papa."

"I don't think so. Remember that time you went to Calcutta? You were thirteen, and you did something none of us could."

"I remember," Anita said, thinking back. "Umang Chacha found Adrith Tauji, and when he said he misses having the paper …" Anita stopped midsentence. It was not safe to talk about Tauji. Rumors floated that he had died when covering riots in Calcutta. Others said he was alive in Burma. The family did nothing to staunch speculation about Adrith's death. It was best if no one knew the truth.

After the Ludlow incident, Ishaan hired new chowkidars. He raised the walls surrounding their house. He could not protect his factories, but his home on East Canal Road would be unassailable. He vacated the third-floor apartment and positioned guns in the windows. One sentry armed with a *durbeen* and whistle was stationed there so anyone approaching the house on East Canal Road from any direction could be surveilled and a signal sent to Munshi Ram, who was given authority to deny entrance to anyone he chose to and open fire if his orders were disobeyed.

Ishaan interviewed every employee but failed to find the informant—probably someone peripheral to the business because the information had been inaccurate. He would have to be more vigilant; that type would grow in numbers as British sanctions tightened and more people went hungry.

Ludlow became a regular visitor. Always police business. He made sure any task having anything to do with the Chands was assigned to him and personally led raids when required.

One day, it was not Ludlow who brought the orders.

The superintendent of police, Dehradun District, sent orders for Chand Publishers to cease operations—no charges noted in the writ.

Anita went to the police station to meet the superintendent. He was not available. The deputy superintendent was also not available.

"Fine. I am going to sit here till someone tells me why my business has been fettered."

Inspector Eric Blair appeared from somewhere in the back. "The injunction came from the highest authorities. We are required to act promptly." Then in an acidic tone, he said, "You should be glad no one in your family was arrested."

"I will not comply with the shutdown order unless given a reason. You can arrest me."

They rewarded Inspector Blair for maintaining order, not rousing natives. He sighed, sat, and feigned sympathy. "There is a blanket ban on publishing. Yours is one name on the list."

"There must be an error." Anita stood. "We publish children's books. We have already been searched by Sergeant Ludlow. Maybe he can tell me what is going on."

"I am afraid that is not possible. Sergeant Ludlow has been transferred to Saharanpur District."

"When did he leave? And why?"

"I am not at liberty to discuss police matters with you, Miss Chand."

There was nothing to be done. Anita exited the compound, lost in thought.

The skinny Indian constable was upon her before she heard his whispers. "*Didi ... Didi ... ruko; ek minute.*"

Anita stopped.

"Are you the one who lives on East Canal Road?" he asked. One hand carried a baton as usual, but the other clutched a sheaf of papers.

"Yes, I am. Do you know me?" He looked familiar, but Anita could not place him.

"No, but I was at your house once." He looked around furtively, making sure no one was looking or close enough to overhear. "Take this."

"What is it?"

"It is for you. From Ludlow sahib." He held the bundle as if handling hot coals. "Take it and put it in your bag."

"Who are you?" Anita hid the papers and waited. The man knew more; he used to accompany the sergeant, she remembered.

"Ludlow sahib is not in Saharanpur. They said that to fool you. Maybe Dilli—for a high-level inquiry. They stripped him of his rank, but he did not care. He said he would have cared if they found out about the box. He led the raid on your factory and destroyed everything except this one manuscript. I have been waiting for a chance to give it to you. I dare not go to your house."

"Have you read it?"

"I don't read English well, but I saw Ludlow sahib poring over it."

"If he ever comes to visit, will you send me word? I won't tell anyone about this."

"I doubt he can return. He disobeyed their command to arrest you for questioning when nothing was found in the raid."

Anita did not care for the expression on the constable's face. She gave him her most formal smile and said, "Shukriya."

Anita hurried home. In bed, she read the passages highlighted in red, and she kissed the first love letter she had ever received, hidden in between the pages. She cried and penned her own letter, recounting how much she had wanted to touch him that first day. He had risked his life and thrown away a career but not in vain, she wrote. She sealed the letter in an envelope and stamped it, though she had no address. She wrote the next night and again the night after that till the pile became too big for the bedside drawer, and so she moved it to her steel almirah, and she continued writing.

After independence in 1948, one hundred imprints of *The India Struggle 1920–1942*, by Subhas Chandra Bose, were printed in her publishing house and gifted to the police.

# 24

*August 1947*

August 15, 1947, dawned bright and beautiful in the Doon Valley. Much the same as the dawn before and the one before that.

No Whites Only clubs were trashed; no police stations mobbed. Church and temple bells tolled as usual; mosques held prayer meetings; gurdwaras served langar lunch to everyone who came.

There was no mass exodus or influx of people—white or brown.

Jawaharlal Nehru's speech, given at midnight, made newspaper headlines. A tryst with destiny is a joy and a responsibility, and it was welcomed with joy and no malice by the Chands of Dehradun. Then on August 17, the Radcliffe line—cleaving one country into two—was revealed. The country shed tears of blood.

"Baoji would have cried today," Leela said. "What the British started with the Bengal Partition they have now extracted as the price of freedom. Is this revenge?"

Samar agreed. "The Raj honed *divide and rule* to a fine art. Afraid of a Hindu majority, they started a census along religious lines and spread lies about our scriptures. They treated us the worst, for employment or business deals, and when incarcerated, Hindus were the most marginalized. This is true not only in India. In South Africa, they fomented hatred among prisoners by prominently displaying disparity in rations meted out by race: chicken for whites, rotis to Indians, and pretty much nothing to natives; they gave whites shoes, Indians chappals, and blacks no footwear. If there was any rioting, it was among the prisoners, and after release, the divisions remained."

"Yes," said Umang. "It was there that Gandhiji started cleaning toilets—to show solidarity with locals since they never assigned such tasks to whites."

"Some white people are good," said Samar, distressed at this latest calamity. "What can we do?"

Ishaan worried too. "The British think India will not survive as an independent nation, that the chaos of partition will give them the power to rule us again. We got independence for a few days in 1946 after the Indian Navy led a revolt, but then we lost it. The same thing could happen again."

"Then we must prove them wrong," said Leela. "I do not know any Muslim family that feels forced to leave Dehradun—especially not among the educated. They are as loyal to India as you or me. We must think. What would Baoji have done in such a situation?"

"Leela is right." Ishaan turned to Samar, who was known to be impartial and respected because he taught children in Leela's school for free. "Samar, people listen to you. It does not matter how we got here, but now we must have peace. There is no room for hatred and revenge against our own people."

"I don't understand why there is such violence among people

who were friends till yesterday. The British are capable of planting traitors among us to incite panic. Could that be the case? We cannot let that happen in Dehradun," Umang agreed. "Hindus and Muslims in the military are united. Civilians can unite too."

"Samar, come with me to the office and reassure all employees they are safe and welcome at our company," said Ishaan. "Our company will uphold Pitaji's ideals, and so will our country. Umang can spread the word at his work."

"Yes. Let us go now before the situation gets worse," Samar agreed. "After that, we can tour the factories so the workers can hear from us directly."

Leela could have hugged her husband but thought better of it; such displays were better saved for nighttime.

"And we can open our home to anyone who needs help—whether leaving or coming to India." Leela held a letter that had come, addressed to Kishan Chand Das, from a name she did not recognize. Hindus fleeing Lahore were going wherever they found contacts. The house on East Canal Road welcomed all who sought shelter on their way to other parts of India or made Dehradun their home.

The Doon Valley saw isolated incidents of unrest, and there were none at any of the Chand factories or offices. But it was not so in the border states of Punjab and Bengal. Many lost families, fortune, and even their lives on the road to freedom.

Delhi too was unsafe with this unexpected blow from the departing viceroy.

Anita helped herself to toast and tea and noticed Papa and Amma were already tucking into aloo-parathas. Samar Tauji and Taiji were arriving. Umang Chacha was nowhere to be seen; he must have already left for the hospital.

She sipped tea and breathed—ahh. "Amma, your tea is the best."

"Not my tea, ours. Dehradun became rich because it had three resources aplenty: chai, *choona*, chawal," Leela corrected. "We grew high-quality tea leaves; our basmati rice sends gourmands into raptures; and the limestone produced from our hills is calcium rich and fetches high prices for all types of construction. Our family owes everything to this land. But it is different now. Chai and choona are gone, and rice fields like ours are disappearing too."

"Ever the teacher! Change is good, Amma. Instead of commodities, we have education—the best military and civilian schools, thanks in no small part to you. I have changed too." Anita waved a piece of paper. "I wrote my first poem last night."

"What is it about?"

"Here. You read it first, Papa." Ishaan was sitting next to Anita. "Then Amma."

He read it and passed it to Leela.

"Leela, you are the teacher. What do you say?"

Leela read out loud:

> Should we spill blood with canons and guns, to deny freedom?
> Should we defy, stand unarmed, nose to nose, to defend freedom,
> Or laugh, raise another pint, to denounce this freedom?
> Should we toil away, night and day, to pay for freedom,
> Or shrug, turn up the volume, and say how empty, senseless is this freedom?
> Should we die in muddy fields to assert our dignity, to reclaim freedom?
> Should we obey the line on a map, written in faraway soil to wreak havoc on freedom?

No matter which side of the battle we fight, no matter how we wage war,
We know what everyone wants is freedom.

Everyone had stopped chewing. Anita looked around. Papa nodded encouragingly, and Tauji clapped. As if resurfacing from deep thought, Amma said, "I think you should write more poems."

"Well, I am glad you like it because I don't think you are going to like what I say next," Anita mumbled.

"Since when has that concerned you?" Leela asked.

"I am going to Delhi tomorrow."

"This is not a good time. Delhi is not safe right now," Ishaan said.

"I have to. I am going to find Sergeant Ludlow."

"Who told you he is in Delhi?" Leela tried to stay calm. "Besides, you do not even know his full name. How will you find him?"

"Don't stop me, Amma. He is in jail because of me. If he had not disobeyed orders to arrest me, I would be in jail today."

"You like him, don't you?" Leela stalled.

"Not all Englishman are bad." Anita turned to her father. "Papa, you won't stop me, will you?"

"His name is Colin. Colin Ludlow," Ishaan said. "I know about the raid and the evidence he removed to save you."

"Oh, Papa!" Anita rose and hugged him. "You kept track. I did not know."

"Of course, I did. I keep score." Ishaan laughed and looked at Leela. "Ask your Amma. She keeps score too."

"Good. Then she can't stop me from going either."

Leela ignored Ishaan and said, "Anita, you know your reason for going; don't pretend it is gratitude. Colin Ludlow would like to see it in your eyes. That is all I am saying."

"Oh, so this isn't about me anymore. Are you talking about

yourself, Amma?" Anita dimpled at her father. "You two act like teenagers. So, are you going to help me, Papa?"

"Do we have a choice?" Leela interrupted. "It seems you have already decided."

"Of course, we will." Ishaan kissed Anita on the forehead and laughed. "You called him *cooler than a cocktail, sharper than a Japanese knife*. I had to keep track. You know all about Japanese knives, but when did you have that cocktail?"

"I love him, Papa. I have to find him."

"Your grandfather would approve. The Chand family always repays their debts. Here is Ludlow's contact information, and I will also give you a letter addressed to my lawyer. Stay safe and bring him home."

# GLOSSARY

(Adapted from Wikipedia: https://www.wikipedia.org/)

**almirah.** A wardrobe, cabinet, or cupboard. Typically, it is not built in but placed in a room like furniture.

**ashram.** A hermitage, monastic community, or other place of religious retreat for Hindus. Ashram first appeared in English in the early 1900s and gained traction after Indian leader Mahatma Gandhi founded his famous ashrams at Sabarmati near Ahmadabad and at Sevagram near Wardha. The word *ashram* derives from a Sanskrit word, "srama," which means "exertion." Later in the twentieth century, English speakers broadened the term *ashram* to encompass any sort of religious retreat, regardless of denomination. In addition to practicing yoga and meditation, a devotee may also receive instruction from a religious teacher and do some type of manual or mental work during their stay at the ashram.

**amma.** Mother. The letters *ji* after a word denote respect.

**baoji, bapji.** Baba or bapu is the root word for father or father-in-law with *ji*.

**belpatra.** Leaf of bel (wood apple). It is offered in prayer rituals, especially to Shiva. This leaf is trifoliate, which signifies the holy Trinity: Brahma, Vishnu, and Shiva. Read more at https://www.boldsky.com/yoga-spirituality/faith-mysticism/2013/importance-of-belpatra-bilva-leaves-036354.html.

**bhai.** Brother.

**charpai.** Lightweight stringed cot, easy to transport.

**choli.** A fitted, blouselike garment worn with a sari.

**coolies.** British word for laborers.

**dai.** Doula.

**dadu.** A variation of *dada*, paternal grandfather. Used by grandchildren to show affection, while a respectful address would be Dadaji.

**diya.** A small oil lamp made from baked clay. Used for prayer or ceremonial occasions.

**dupatta.** A length of material worn as a scarf or head covering, typically with a salwar-kurta outfit, by women from South Asia. A dupatta is traditionally worn across both shoulders in the front and drapes in the back.

**fakir.** An ascetic, wise man who gives up material things in pursuit of spiritual enlightenment. They sometimes set up temporary shelter on the way to a shrine, and pilgrims passing by offer food and flowers in homage.

**ghat.** A series of steps leading to a body of water, particularly a holy river. Used by bathers to reach the water. The set of stairs can lead to something as small as a pond or as large as a major river. The numerous significant ghats along the Ganges are known generally as the Varanasi ghats and the ghats of the Ganges. Some say these were constructed under the patronage of Maratha rulers, such as Ahilyabai Holkar, in the eighteenth century (https://en.wikipedia.org/wiki/Ghat#cite_note-2), while others say they have been there in one form or another since historical times, since Varanasi is considered the (arguably) oldest, living, modern city.

**grihastha.** Householder. One of the four stages of life.

**kurta.** A loose, typically collarless, knee-length shirt worn by men and women from South Asia. Fashion designers nowadays make kurtas in all shapes, lengths, and styles for women. The term *kameez* may also be used interchangeably with kurta.

**mangalsutra.** A necklace worn by a married woman. It may be as simple as a thick thread or a thin gold chain with pendants signifying ancestry. The other common design is alternating tiny gold and black beads. It is designed to be comfortable so it can be worn all the time, like a wedding band in Western tradition.

**mela.** Festival.

**mithai.** Sweetmeat. An item of confectionery or sweet food. Indian dessert.

**monsoon.** In India and nearby lands, the season during which the 'southwest monsoon' blows, commonly marked by heavy rains, rainy season.

**namaste.** Hindi. A respectful greeting common in India. It is used both for salutation and valediction. Namaste is usually spoken with a slight bow and hands pressed together, palms touching and fingers pointing upwards, thumbs close to the chest. Sometimes spoken as namaskar, *namaskaram* in the Sanskrit form.

**papa, pappa.** Informal for father, like dad. Pita or pitaji is formal.

**pakwan.** Sweets made for ceremonial occasions.

**palloo, pallu.** Cloth that drapes over the shoulder. It is part of the garment worn by women in India. See *sari.* May serve to cover the head when required.

**raja (or maharaja).** King (or great king). On the eve of independence in 1947, India (including present-day Pakistan and Bangladesh) contained more than six hundred princely states, each with its own native ruler, often styled raja or rana or thakur (if the ruler was Hindu) or nawab (if he was Muslim). The British directly ruled two-thirds of India; the rest was under indirect rule by the princes under the influence of British representatives. After independence, most were either given respectable positions (governorship of their state) or became politicians.

**sabha.** Political conclave or gathering.

**sari.** A garment worn by women from the Indian subcontinent. It is a cloth drape varying from five to nine yards (4.5 meters to 8 meters) in length and two to four feet (60 cm to 1.20 m) in breadth that is typically wrapped around the waist (tucked into an undergarment called petticoat), with one end draped over the shoulder, called *palloo*, covering the breasts. It is worn with an upper garment usually called blouse or choli. Saris can be very expensive or low priced, and the cloth can vary from silk to cotton or muslin and nowadays nylon.

**swami.** A Hindu ascetic or religious teacher.

**theka.** Lease.

**thali.** Gold, silver, or steel platter.

**vibhuti.** Sanskrit. Sacred ash. It is a gray powder used in holy rituals by priests. It is the ash formed by burning wood (often mango) and camphor and can be bought by devotees along with other offerings for prayer.

# ABOUT THE AUTHOR

Before she turned to writing fiction, Neerja Raman was a scientist. Her research in digital imaging and printing led to collaborations with universities, startups, and government agencies. It motivated her first book, *The Practice and Philosophy of Decision Making: A Seven Step Spiritual Guide*, a leadership framework featured as WITI's Books that Empower Women expo. Raman was inducted into the Women in Technology International (WITI) Hall of Fame and named to Silicon Valley Business Journal's Fifty Most Influential Women list. As digital media became ubiquitous, Raman shifted her research to enabling education and healthcare delivery, using digital content to reduce cost and increase outreach. The humor in pitfalls of balancing a career and raising three children in fast-paced Silicon Valley, informs her fiction debut, *Moments in Transition: Stories of Maya and Jeena*. It was awarded Honorable Mention, by Writer's Digest, and named Finalist by International Book Awards, and by Best Book Awards. She has authored book-chapters, technical papers, essays, short stories, and maintains three blogs.

Raman was born in India and came to New York for graduate studies. She lives in the San Francisco Bay Area. When asked about her writing philosophy, she quotes: Life isn't about how to survive the storm, but how to dance in the rain. Visit her at neerjaraman.com.

# PRAISE

for

Moments in Transition:
Stories of Maya and Jeena

"At times **heartbreaking and at others humorous**, Raman has written a book that just about any reader could relate to in one way or another. And **yet, there is a distinct cultural appeal that both intrigues** those of us less familiar with Indian tradition and manages to connect the characters in their similar experiences, creating an analogy for readers who have experience with other cultures."

– Writer's Digest, Honorable Mention

"Neerja Raman's fiction debut leads us to brilliant and poignant conclusion with an infectious, engaging writing style. She has woven together stories of India and America with effortless grace."

– Sylvia E. Halloran, winner Independent Thinking Essay Contest, Barner and Noble

"Neerja Raman uses eloquent vocabulary and expression to make a personal connection with her reader. Once Upon a River evoked the same feelings in me as Jeena; as if they belong to me as well."

—Manjula Pal, Journalist, Author of Who Wants to Marry a Mama's Boy

# PRAISE

for

The Practice and Philosophy of Decision Maling: A Seven Step Spiritual Guide

"An intriguing and original reading of the Gita as a guide to practical decision-making.... A thought provoking and instructive book."

–Shashi Tharoor, Author and former United Nations Under Secretary General

"Neerja is a technical leader, a civic leader, a working mom, a mentor, and a friend to many. Her values-based framework grows out of and informs giving new meaning to 'work life balance'. This book is engaging and easy to read. The tools continuously help me make tough choices and tradeoffs for a fulfilling life at work, at home, and in my community."

–Brabara Waugh, Author and co-founder, World Inclusion, Hewlett Packard

"I enjoyed reading the book. The words come from a certain inspiration and conviction, it seems to me...Stories like the one on Two Cats and The Happy Man make the reading quite delightful... The section on six kinds of emotional traps and how to handle them at the end of the book add value to the work. Quotations from Gandhi, Goethe, Swami Chinmayananda, and Pascal have enriched the book."

–Swami Chidananda

CPSIA information can be obtained
at www.ICGtesting.com
Printed in the USA
LVHW052015180123
737396LV00002B/152